The Last Fairy: Uriel's Gift

A Tiny Tale of Magic and Murder

By

Donovan Galway

Deep Indigo Books
Published by Indigo Sea Press
Winston-Salem

Deep Indigo Books
Indigo Sea Press
302 Ricks Drive
Winston-Salem, NC 27103

First Deep Indigo Books edition published
January, 2016
Deep Indigo Books, Moon Sailor and all production design are trademarks of Indigo Sea Press, used under license.

For information regarding bulk purchases of this book, digital purchase and special discounts, please contact the publisher at indigoseapress.com

Editing by Tracy Fabre
Cover design by Donovan Galway

Manufactured in the United States of America
ISBN 978-1-63066-263-9

To my amazing wife, Karen
for the faith, the inspiration
and for the magic she brings
into my life.

The First Chapter

Miguel Urenda held his blade. The dense forest just a few meters ahead posed no obstacle for the massive bulldozer beneath him. With a simple motion of his hand he could advance and level a broad path through the jungle with relative ease, but he remained still. Directly in his path, a marsh deer stood equally still and stared back.

"It's the one on the right!" The voice on his radio pulled a portion of his attention from the unnatural display of defiance. Failing to fully blink himself out of his trance, Miguel reached for the microphone.

"*Que?*"

"The accelerator. Did you forget how to drive that dozer?"

"No. I mean... There's animals here, boss."

"What animals?"

"This deer. It's looking right at me. They were supposed to clear the wildlife." He remained mesmerized by the vision. The statuesque and elegant marsh deer was normally too cunning to come this close to man and generally stayed near the rivers and streams, though the rampant encroachment of earth-leveling machines had disrupted the ecosystem here beyond recognition. Still, it was less the presence of this wary doe than the strange halo of light surrounding her which held Miguel frozen at the controls. The odd luminescence seemed to emit a hue he had never seen before. It was at once red and blue, yet neither, not blended to purple but a strangely unnatural color.

"Yeah well, the higher-ups figured they could kill two birds with one bulldozer and save a few pesos. Is that a problem?"

"No. No, Boss. No problem." He responded as he knew he should, but with only half his heart in it. The rest was being pulled into the hypnotic light show before him.

"Okay. So get rolling. Don't worry about Bambi. You couldn't catch that thing if you wanted to. Now get it in gear."

The increasingly angry tone in his foreman's voice brought Miguel back to reality. Seventy-five percent of the workforce was American, and almost no locals actually handled machinery. He was happy to have been chosen to work on Phase Four, which cleared the ancient rainforest. Two miles behind him, Phase Three was already planted with straight rows of seedling palm trees. Phase Two was beyond, with nearly mature palms ready to yield the precious palm oil. Miguel was fluent in English and experienced in operating heavy machinery, so when the company fell under pressure to hire at least a few locals in some capacity, he was an ideal public relations candidate. He knew he was fortunate to hold this relatively high-paying position, and he owed it to his wife and children to move his bulldozer into the forest. But this lone barrier stood in his path, and he felt powerless to move against it.

"Move it!" shouted his foreman, and the startled driver pushed the lever forward. The deer leapt away into the protection of the forest, but the luminous aura remained. To Miguel's amazement the glow was not emanating from the animal, but from the forest floor behind it. The hypnotic phenomenon remained in his path, glowing ever brighter.

"Do you see that?" Miguel asked the microphone.

"See what? The deer's gone. Start knocking down the trees."

Miguel rested his hand on the control lever, but could not bring himself to move forward. He sat frozen, his eyes fixed on the glowing life ahead of his bulldozer. The sparks which seemed at first to be flying from the light were actually pouring into it from all directions. As the tiny sparks of light came together, the mass grew in strength and brilliance. It seemed to be drawing Miguel in as well. He could feel the natural energy permeating his body. He could taste it, and he almost believed he could hear it calling to him. The sensation was one of warmth and of reciprocated love, and he felt a smile tugging at the corners of his mouth.

Suddenly a massive tree crashed to the ground atop the glow. The felled giant carried a ton of dying vines, plants and moss and crushed all beneath it. The light was gone.

The driver in the dozer to Miguel's left pushed on with no regard for the tree that had fallen to the side. It was just one of thousands to be cleared, and work was to be done. But the intrusion left Miguel with an odd sense of emptiness. The euphoric warmth he'd felt just seconds before had so completely permeated his body that when it left, he felt nearly nothing. He sat emotionless and drained, as though his heart had been taken from him and thrown beneath the cold weight of the fallen tree. As he pushed forward the control levers to power his machine into the jungle, he tried to remember why he had felt any reluctance. He could only remember caring that his family would go hungry should he hesitate, but even that motivation was no more than a memory, empty and as two-dimensional as the seemingly lifeless world before him.

Miguel drove on as he was ordered, oblivious to the devastation he left in his wake.

*****

The earth teemed with gray, smoldering vapors that wafted over a scorched, desolate surface. There was no sign of life: no birds, no plants, no people. On a distant hill, the noxious air parted, and a beacon of blue reached up and through the ashes and pollution. The ray of light and purity reached to the whitening clouds and spread down the slopes of the hill to reveal a small tree blossoming on a field of green grass. A young girl stood near the tree. She looked directly at the source and took a deep breath. Then she smiled.

As the close-up revealed the clean face of an adorable child, the voice-over carried a soothing tone. "This is not the time to live in denial. We can't afford to dwell on the past. Planetary Power is looking ahead with pride and confidence, not with apologies or excuses, but with answers that make sense, because she needs room to breathe, and a chance to live." The child looked up toward a clear blue sky as her face broke into a broader, heart-warming smile. Looking down, she drew a deep, comfortable breath and sighed in exhale. The image faded to a corporate logo as the voice-over concluded. "Planetary Power Corporation, a division of

Global Nortatem, committed to clean, renewable energy for a future we can live with."

The ad campaign was aimed at gaining the confidence of an increasingly cynical public. The environmental groups were doing such a tremendous job of educating everyone about what was going on that virtually any energy or chemical company was painted with a villainous brush. Though most energy companies were making visible gestures aimed at presenting an environmental awareness, Global meant to be the first to step away from the public judgment and show itself in a believably positive light. They would be the one bucking the odds, taking the losses and making the sacrifices to see that the future was sound. They publicly challenged all oil and gas companies to allocate a percentage of their annual profits toward research and development of new energy sources and to repairing the damage already done to the earth. The campaign, a multi-billion dollar gamble, relied on the company being ready for a major transformation.

The launch party was a massive success. Executives toasted vice presidents. Vice presidents whispered to presidents about them, and CEOs mingled with the masses, pretending to be ordinary employees though none dared address them as such. Everyone was present. Even the faces only seen on corporate newsletters were there, boasting smiles well beyond any seen at any obligatory Christmas party.

Karen Gabriel walked through the crowd accepting handshakes and congratulations from everyone. She seemed even more prominent than the highest level figureheads. Few among them had escaped her drive and zeal over the past several months while the young executive pulled together the biggest merger in corporate history. Under the public blanket of their environmental ad campaign, five energy providers signed contracts with four conglomerate developers who had been granted exclusive clearing rights to undeveloped land by the governments of Indonesia and Columbia. Each deal was contingent on another, and none would sign first. It was three times the kind of transaction that would burst the ulcer of stronger, more seasoned and deal-experience hardened veterans. Sleeping with the phone in one hand, the Blackberry in the other while the laptop updated spreadsheets and market reports for months on end was more than could be asked of any one person. But Karen had gained the trust of government officials on three continents and knew going in which contractors were big enough to take the load and just corrupt enough to be discreet about the promises made.

She had promised to bring it in before the end of the first quarter, and one week early she watched the ink dry on the last contract. She had even found time to oversee the launch of the advertising campaign, designed as a pre-emptive strike against environmental concerns. The acceptance of the corporate world was not enough. She had to have the acceptance of the public as well. Before they could be labeled the bad guys, she would have them painted as the ones who would step away from the strip-miners and environmental terrorists. PPC was going to save the human race. The ad campaign said it so clearly and convincingly that even she believed it.

The glass of champagne that had been pushed into her hand and clinked by countless others had yet to touch her lips. Despite her convincing smile and casual swagger, she was not yet ready to drop the baton. Her mind had been racing twenty-four hours a day for what seemed a professional lifetime, juggling every issue great and small regarding the merger. Now she stood at the finish line, the tape and victory within her grasp. All she had to do was stop thinking about it and take a drink. Just like that. Just stop thinking about it. Simply turn it off. Stop the wheels. There was nothing left to do. Yet her glass remained full.

The crowd seemed to part before her. Her legal advisor and chief contract consultant Millburn Jenkins was first to impede her ascent from entrance to exit. He gave her the reassuring smile which had become his word to her that he'd managed to do what she wanted, and it was as profitable as she'd hoped. Millburn willingly worked under her despite being vastly more experienced and possibly the smartest and shrewdest man she'd ever known. His trademark smile had become almost frequent in recent weeks. Karen took this one as a farewell smile. She hoped to prolong her farewell a bit longer and politely turned away from him.

As she turned, her eyes fell upon a tall, sandy-haired man smiling at her from across the room. His face was so sincere it brought sincerity to hers. She smiled back at him. The man lifted his glass to her in salute, and Karen found herself reciprocating. Together, separated by an empty floor, they toasted her, and Karen finally tasted the sweet champagne of her success. She swallowed and felt it roll down her throat. The exhale that followed was the first she was aware of for months, and it had been drawn out of her by a total stranger. She felt an immediate connection with him. Her usual wariness was gone, and he seemed to have with only a glance penetrated all of her barriers. Why, she wondered, had she allowed this man in? What did he want of her, and why was she tempted to surrender it?

Two biologists from her lab team came to join her in the toast and revel in the glory. Their voices pierced the walking daydream she had been drifting through, and she blinked as if suddenly awakening. As they spoke, Karen tried to peer between them at the smiling stranger. The crowd was in a constant state of intermixing, and she could not find the fellow again. No matter, she thought. He would surely turn up.

"You just don't look like you're having a good time," said a familiar voice from over her left shoulder. Karen turned to find agent Jim Gunn standing close enough to hug had he chosen to do so. "If you don't loosen up, I'll be forced to file a suspicious activity report."

"Agent Gunn. Finally taking a day off?"

Jim brandished the youthful smile that belied his experience and dedication. "The bad guys never take a day off. Neither does the FBI."

"Really?"

"Actually document crime is off all the time. I think that's the only part of it I'll miss."

"You're leaving the bureau?"

Jim shook his head as far as he could while sipping his champagne. "Moving up. Apparently all the background checks I did for your project, tedious as it was, drew some high profile attention. I'm finally moving up to field agent."

"I can't picture you with a gun in your hand."

"Tragically, it's not likely to happen. Most of what we do now is in research. The difference will be subtle, but the title is slightly more impressive. I owe that to you."

"Not at all, Jim. We literally couldn't have done it without you. Thank you."

"Well, I'm still downtown. If you ever need anything, and I mean anything, give me a call. Code name Lemondrop."

Karen nearly spurted her drink. "Lemondrop?"

"I know. It doesn't exactly strike fear in the heart, does it? Oh well."

*****

One thousand, six hundred and eleven miles northeast of the celebration, Melvin Dinsdale sat on a bridge over the Chicago River. The service indent allowed him enough space to sit out of the path of the occasional jogger and shield himself from the relentless wind. Winter was long over in most areas of the country, but here, near the Canadian border, the cold and damp clung tenaciously to life, seeking unprotected souls to touch and wound. Melvin felt the cold and minded it very much, though it had been more years than he cared to recount since he had anyone to whom he might voice his objection. He pulled his rags closer to his neck in defense.

He could hear the voices of two men approaching. He could not be bothered to try to make out the words, though their tone told him they were not intent on passing him by. As his collar protected him from the weather, his lowered eyes and motionless poise were his defenses against those who would speak to him or judge him. They served with equal ineffectiveness.

The two men stopped and hunkered down near Melvin.

7

One of them placed a caring hand on his shoulder.

"I want you to come over to the shelter with us."

Melvin shook his head without looking up to them. "Ain't goin' in there."

"Just for one night. Have something to eat. Sleep in a bed. Let a doctor have a look at you."

"Ain't goin' in there."

The other man spoke in a more assertive voice. "If you stay out here, you're going to die. You know that?"

"That's what you told me in the winter. Didn't die."

"You will."

"So will you. I'll be right here doing what I want."

"You can do what you want in there. You just won't get rained on while you do it."

"The shelter's right there! Just go in, for God's sake, man."

"I go in there, they'll all be tellin' me what to do, where to sit, what to call them. Ain't doin' it. No sir."

The two men stood and looked at each other in exasperation. One looked down at the pile of rags. "We close the doors at ten, but you can come in anytime you want."

"And leave as easily," said the other. "I promise no one will try to stop you." He watched the rags for an acknowledgement that was not to come. Having done what he came for, he and his partner surrendered to the stronger will and returned to the homeless shelter.

Melvin listened to their footfalls vanishing to leave him in his solitude. He did not hear the new set of shoes approach until their wearer stood before him. Melvin looked up into a pair of kind eyes. The man smiled down at him, but not in the mocking or pitying manner he had become accustomed to. The expression, as best he could define it from memory, was one of admiration. He returned with one of bewildered awe.

"They didn't seem to want to take no for an answer," the man said.

"They never do. But it's all I got for them."

The man looked out across the river. "Not a bad night."

"Seen worse."

"I'll bet. Last winter must have been a real bitch."

Melvin snickered. "Last winter was a week ago. Where you been?"

"Indoors. But hey. As long as you're happy. You are happy. Aren't you?"

Melvin looked up at the sandy-haired man with eyes that belied the desperation of his situation. "You could say that."

The man seemed to like the answer. His grin broadened enough to display a deep dimple in his left cheek. "I know the feeling. Those fellows only want to help. But they think what makes them happy is the only thing that can make anybody happy. Me? I like vanilla ice cream. That's all. No nuts. Maybe some chocolate syrup but I don't need it. Just plain vanilla ice cream. But you know, every time I eat it, somebody tries to tell me I should put something on it. Whipped cream or fudge or nuts or another flavor. Why is it so hard for them to understand that I just like vanilla ice cream? No nuts. Just vanilla. Just let me alone to eat it in peace."

Melvin was watching the man speak. "Mister, that's probably the smartest thing I ever heard. You some kind of preacher or something?"

"Not me. If I was, I'd be looking for souls that needed saving. You look like you've found your peace, friend."

"I have. That I have."

"I envy you. Can I ask? Where did you find it?"

Melvin touched his chest over his rag-covered heart. "Right here."

The man smiled a saintly smile and said, "Bullshit. You can sit there shivering with the cold and bent over half from hunger and half from the garbage you had for supper yesterday and tell me you're happy? Nope. Something makes you happy. Something that makes all this bearable. You've got something... special. Don't you? Share it with me. I won't take it. I just want to know."

He looked down at Melvin with anticipation and hope. But as Melvin looked up, the inquisitive stranger saw a light go out in his eyes. The pleasant stare faded to blankness as though he had forgotten who was speaking. He rewound to the beginning and was now looking up at a total stranger for the first time. He didn't know this stranger. He didn't like him. The stranger would likely tell him to go into the shelter. They all did. Melvin Dinsdale lowered his eyes and pulled his collar against the cold.

The man watched Melvin shun him as he would anyone. The answer he needed wasn't here, and time was too precious to be spent here. As he turned to leave, Melvin looked up as if suddenly realizing something of some importance. The man stayed and dared hope.

"Hey," Melvin said. "Ain't you... Ice Cream?"

The stranger smiled at the futility of his own hopes. "That's right, friend. I'm Ice Cream. And you're Nuts." Certain there were no secrets to be revealed, he turned away. Whatever Melvin had was locked away for good.

The Second Chapter

Marian Rimsburg was not expected to recover. The triple bypass was risky considering her declining years, and she developed pneumonia within hours of being closed. Her family in some form or measure was ever present, waiting for news, but no one of the hospital staff dared give them any hope. The responses to the family's queries ranged from delays and promises to check to assurances that all things happen for a reason, and she would want them to be strong.

The waiting room that evening held Marian's eldest son Paul and his younger sister Louise, Louise's husband Andrew and two children. The children were tired of being there and long since bored with the books and toys set about. When Dr. Harvey entered the waiting room brandishing his official-looking chart, they all felt the end of their sojourn was near.

Dr. Harvey made a brief eye contact with everyone before clearing his throat. "Mr. Rimsburg? Would you like the good news or the bad news?"

Paul looked at Louise to see if she seemed annoyed with the poor taste of the question. Assuming the worst as he had prepared himself for, he responded. "What's the bad news, Doc?"

"There is none. Your mother has come out of her fever and is asking for a Braunschweiger sandwich. Anyone know what that is?"

Louise smiled. "It's blood sausage. It's disgusting, but she must be feeling better."

Marian had astonished the hospital staff with a miraculous recovery. In less than an hour, her fever dissipated to nearly normal. The fluid in her lungs was gone, and the remaining infection was easily treatable with antibiotics. Marian went from deathbed to happy discharge in record time. As her family members willingly wheeled Marian out to the waiting van to taxi her home again, it was evident to all watching that a lion's share of joy was held by

Marian. Her children seemed to wear forced smiles that vanished anytime they looked at each other.

She waved enthusiastic goodbyes to everyone as she was wheeled through the quiet hospital. The nurses waved back and offered simple words of support. The doctors gave thumbs up and encouraging gestures. The tall, sandy-haired man in the lobby smiled as she waved to him like a family member. She had no idea how much her recovery interested him or why.

The nurse left her just inside the door and went to prepare her ride. The tall man stepped up and bent at her side. "That was some recovery, Marian. How did you do it?"

Marian had become accustomed to strangers talking to her, asking things of her, sticking things in her. It was a hospital, where social rules rarely apply, so she thought little of this gentleman's query. "Well, it was just a miracle. The doctors and nurses here have been so fantastic, but I think someone was just watching over me."

"I think so, too. Who do you...?"

At that moment the nurse returned and pulled her out through the automatic doors. He watched quietly as she was loaded into her van. Marian waved to everyone, including the concerned stranger, as her ride pulled away.

He watched her drive on to her family and the rest of her life. She might have what he sought, but something was missing. Time was running out, and there were so many people to watch, so many events to investigate. The stranger knew he would be back when it was time, or when time was up.

The happy Rimsburg family façade lasted less than a week. It was an otherwise typical afternoon in the neighborhood as the neighbors came out to witness the spectacle unfolding.

Louise lunged at one of the social workers on her porch. Had her husband not caught her, the police officer was prepared to defend himself. They had come unannounced with a warrant to remove the children from their home pending an investigation, though they would give very few details in front of the children.

"There's been a report filed, and we have to investigate it. That's all we can tell you at this stage, Mrs. Barnett," the social worker stated in a cold, smug voice.

"You heartless bitch!" Louise shouted at her. "How can you come here and steal my children and then dare to speak to me in that tone? Give me my children!"

Andrew maintained his hold on her but was no more sympathetic. "How can you just take our children away? What are we supposed to have done? Who filed the charges?"

"I'm sure you understand we can't divulge that at this time. You'll get a full explanation at the hearing."

The officer ushered them to the side of the porch just as the door opened. Two more case workers carried the children out of the house. They cried for their mother and reached for her, but she was held firm.

"No! For God's sake no!" Louise begged. "My babies!"

"Please just let us say goodbye," Andrew pleaded. "They're our children."

The officer holding them back showed no sympathy, nor did the caseworker as she made notes in her binder. "Well, you should have thought of that before."

"Before what?"

The woman looked up at the officer. "They've been served, Officer, thank you. Just be sure we get away safely." Then she turned without another word to the sobbing parents. The children had been loaded into a black SUV. As the case worker opened her door to get in, the children's cries became louder, then muffled again as the door closed.

Louise was nearly hysterical as the SUV pulled away. Behind it, she and Andrew saw Marian sitting in her own car with a vindictive sneer.

"You did this!" Louise shouted at her. "You finally did it! You lied to them. Didn't you? You horrible old hag!"

"Why?" Andrew shouted at her, still held at bay by the vigilant policeman. "Why would you take our kids?"

Marian did not bother to respond. The lies she had told to Child Protective Services were complex enough to be plausible and sordid enough to draw immediate attention.

13

Donovan Galway

She knew children were sometimes afraid to tell of the dark things that happen after the lights go out. CPS had almost come to take a denial from a child as a confirmation. Whether yes or no, they removed the children from danger so as not to be accused of inaction. This time they acted, and Marian would be there to confirm what she "had been told" by her grandchildren. They would be remanded into her custody with the added support of a restraining order. After all, she thought, she was the only one who knew how to take care of them. With the plan underway, she made no attempt to conceal the smile of satisfaction as she started off.

As her car pulled away, she noticed a man standing on the sidewalk looking directly at her. Many of the neighbors had come out to gawk at them, but this man looked oddly familiar. She could not quite place the tall stranger. At the hospital perhaps. His expression was less of disgust or condemnation than of disappointment. No matter. She had her grandchildren at last, and her life was perfect.

The tall stranger watched in total dejection as she drove off. She was clearly not the one he was looking for.

The Third Chapter

Karen sat in her office staring at the phone. She was trying to remember the last time there were absolutely no messages on it, and she truly was not sure how to react. All of her duties and responsibilities had been centered on the merger for so long that she literally had nothing else to do. This was a frightening revelation for a devout work addict.

Her computer alerted her to an incoming E-mail, and she nearly lunged at the keyboard. The message from her boss was titled "Urgent concern." She clicked on it and read:

"What are you doing here? You're supposed to be home packing. Go. Pack. Leave. Relax. Order. Vic."

Thinking as hard as she could about the merger project, Karen fought to think of a loose end or detail missed. As had always been her trademark, every detail down to the postage had been assigned to a responsible person at hand over. The project was running smoothly, and as she had left instructions to contact her if anything needed attention, and no one had attempted to contact her, she was left with the post-project depression syndrome. She had never encountered this syndrome to this degree, but she was confident it could only be resolved by an extreme reversal, meaning a vacation in Barbados or another project.

Projects had always been brought to her for execution. She had never had to go out and look for work and had little idea where to begin. The thought process was surely first. She had to think. Just think. Karen found it odd that the simple act of thinking clearly on a subject of any real magnitude seemed difficult. Her mind continually wandered to less significant matters. Her shoes were too tight. What do people wear in Barbados? Had she paid her electric bill? Wouldn't a hand be better if the pinky finger had evolved into another thumb? Before she could again shake herself back to the mental state she demanded of herself, another E-mail came through.

"I know you see this, and I know you're still here. Vic."

Vic Albean sat in his office staring at his computer with a level of intensity Karen had seen in few people other than herself. She pushed her head farther inside the door. "Got a minute?"

Vic seemed to find it difficult to divert his attention from the screen. "Uh huh. What's up?"

"If you're busy I can... Is that anything I can help with?"

"Why would you want to help Oprah?"

Puzzled, Karen came around the desk and looked at his screen. He was watching Oprah Winfrey on his computer.

"Did you know you could get television on these things?" Vic asked.

"Since when is daytime television part of your job description?"

The distraction seemed to cause Vic to lose interest, and he clicked the program off, looking up at her as though he had just realized she was in the room. "Hi there."

She was taken aback by the uncharacteristically flippant attitude of the normally driven executive. "Um... Hi? What's up, Vic?"

"Oh nothing. I got an E-mail from the directors wanting to know when you land in Barbados."

"The directors? Why do they care what I do with my spare time?"

"Don't know. Don't care. Didn't you get my E-mail?"

"You've been sending me twenty a day for eighteen months."

"But how many this week?"

"I saw it. It can wait."

Vic handed her an envelope. "The tickets are non-refundable. I want you on a plane to Barbados and topless on a beach by Friday. That's probably an order."

Karen barely glanced at the tickets and printed itinerary. "I don't do topless."

"I'll settle for barefoot, but the rest is non-negotiable. Get out of here and take some time off." He turned away and peered out the large window, staring wistfully at the view.

His attitude was so far displaced from what she had worked with and around for months that she was given pause to think. Her mental placement, too, had been a bit off track lately. Something was different, and she was unsure how it would end up. This left her with a sense of being controlled rather than in control. It was not her, and she forced herself to try to take charge of it. Of something.

"Vic. Do you have any idea what we'll be doing when I get back?" Her boss seemed unable to keep his focus on her and away from the window, though he could see nothing but clouds. She tried again to gain his attention. "What's next, Vic? Vic? Hello? Are you in there?"

"Um… sure. We have a five-year lease on it."

"On what?"

"The hotel. It's all comped, so go and try to relax. Have a Mai Tai or whatever they're drinking these days."

Karen realized he was hopelessly distracted. There had been an enormous emotional release since the launch of the merger. Everyone involved seemed to be reacting differently. But Vic was usually more driven than even Karen. The workaholic blood they shared was the primary reason she was headhunted by him and promoted so rapidly. They spoke the same language. Now he seemed uncharacteristically bent on drifting away. Karen had not been comfortable with this kind of attitude since high school. She elected to give him the rein and take some time away from him. She could still work if that was how she relaxed. She would simply work on a laptop poolside in Barbados. How could any corporate executive object to that?

"When do I leave?"

"Day after tomorrow. Call the airline and give them your details. Get a tan and a smile before you come back. That's an order… or something." He was only half with her. Mentally he was still drawn to a cloud that resembled Richard Nixon. It was as if nothing inside the building was of any real interest to him.

Karen let him wander out before she muttered, "I don't do barefoot."

The Fourth Chapter

"Hey, Blue!" Will Billings called out to the umpire. "Good game out there! You ought to watch it!"

The softball umpire was not offended or even distracted by the time-honored taunt. He simply took his position near third base and signaled to his partner behind the plate that he was ready for the next batter.

Ten-year-old Megan Dunbar stepped up to the plate. Meagan Stanley was on deck waiting her turn. With only one out and no one on base, she was assured an at-bat, and she was on a streak. Her father had promised her a new cell phone if she got one more stand-up double.

Will studied the infield as if it mattered and shouted encouragement to the new batter. "All right, Megan!" The batter, the on-deck Meagan and five more girls in his dugout turned to him. "Dunbar!" he shouted for clarification, and the other Megans looked away. "Just look it in." He knew this pitcher. Brittany James was eleven and pitching well above her station. She was the only pitcher in the eleven and under league with three pitches. Most only threw the ball and hoped for a strike. They all called this their fastball. Brittany had an effective fastball, a change-up and drop curve that was actually difficult to hit.

Brittany took a signal from her catcher and threw a perfect strike. Megan swung and missed, and her coach was quick to shout encouragement. "All right, Meg. No problem. Look for the stitches on the ball." He had taught his team to look for the stitching on the ball as it was coming in. They could actually tell which way the ball was spinning. That didn't matter as much as the concentration it took to see the stitches. If they were looking that hard, their slugging percentage soared.

Meagan Stanley leaned back against the chain link fence as she waited her turn. Inside the dugout, Rena James looked at the blonde ponytail pressed against the fence and could not resist a prank. She pulled a roll brush from her bat bag and carefully pulled Meagan's hair through the diamond opening in the fence. Shushing her teammates, she quickly rolled the hair up into the brush, pinning her teammate to the fence.

Rena knew this would tangle the girl's hair. She had no idea to what extent it would hurt and resist untangling. Meagan screamed and pulled against the brush, tightening the snare. One of the parents was always in the dugout as an assistant to watch the girls. The "Dugout Mom," as the position had been dubbed, was first to come to her aid. Her friends rushed to try and unravel the hair, but the panicking hands worsened the situation and further terrified the girl.

Her cries halted the game as Will and Meagan's parents came to try to help. Rena moved as far away from the commotion as possible, but she had committed the crime before too many witnesses.

"What the heck's wrong with these kids, Billings?" Meagan's father demanded.

"Sorry, Ted. I can't hold all their hands. I'm out on the field. John?" he called to the dugout mom. "What happened?"

"You're responsible for them!" Mr. Stanley shouted.

"Well, what am I supposed to do?"

"Well, do something!"

The umpire came up to the screen and saw them desperately trying to free the player. "Can she go, Coach?"

"We're a little busy now, Ben. Can you give us a minute?" He was doing his best to keep the girl calm and motionless while her mother picked at her hair. The weeping girl clearly was not going to bat.

"You've got a minute, Coach. Then you'll have to scratch her."

"I don't care!" Meagan shouted.

Will cared not only for the girl, but for her importance in the line-up. His roster was already short, and if he pulled her, he wouldn't have enough to play. He looked at the bench. He had one viable substitute, and that was Rena. She sat in the corner of the dugout and fought against giggling over her mischievous prank. She had been benched for missing practice and was not supposed to play today. Now she thought she just might. Although the prank was not intended to take Meagan out of the line-up, she would take it as a bonus.

Will refused to reward her for the devious act. He looked her directly in the eye and said, "Feryl! On deck!"

Rena and the rest of the team looked to the other side of the bench. Feryl was Will's daughter. Frail and small for her age, she rarely played, though she never missed practice. The girls liked her somewhat, but knew she could barely hold the bat, let alone help her team. Will had built the team for her and tried to avoid putting her in embarrassing situations, but he needed her now. Rena was clearly annoyed with the call, so he knew it was the right one. Feryl would bat.

Feryl reached into her bat bag and pulled out a batting helmet, an aluminum bat and a bottle of hair conditioner. She had to push past the antiseptic hand wipes, surgical masks and shampoo. As she went toward the fence, she handed the bottle to Meagan's mother. "Rinse her hair with this and the brush should roll out. Don't pull it. Just let it slide loose."

"Thank you, Feryl," Mrs. Stanley said in a calm voice. As she worked the lubricant into her daughter's ponytail, she spoke to Will. "Sorry I yelled at you, Will. I know you can't be everywhere. She's quite a girl, that one."

Will thanked her and took his place at third base. He tried not to notice how Feryl's helmet was clearly too large for her. He focused on Megan as she stepped back into the batter's box.

Brittany delivered another fastball that caught Megan looking. "Strike two!" the umpire said.

"Shake it off, Meg!" Will shouted. "Look it in!"

Feryl watched the pitcher take the ball back from the catcher. She studied Brittany fingering the ball in her glove. "Megan!" she called to her teammate. Again all of the Megans on her team turned to her, and she waved them off and pointed to the batter.

Megan turned to look and Feryl gestured to her to move

20

up toward the pitcher. Megan moved a few inches, and Feryl urged her to move more. She held up her hands two feet apart to demonstrate how far she wanted her to move. Megan looked at Will, who nodded in agreement though he truly had no idea what Feryl was thinking. Megan moved up to the front of the batter's box and well out in front of the plate.

Brittany delivered the next pitch which, by history, should have been a change-up that would drop out of the strike zone. A wary batter would hold her bat. But Brittany sent a potentially devastating drop curve that came in hard and dropped just after it crossed the front of the plate. An extremely difficult pitch to hit unless the batter caught it before it dropped. Megan was in perfect position and ripped it between the third baseman and shortstop. She made it safely to second, and her new phone was assured. The team cheered wildly, but she waved gratitude to Feryl.

Now it was Feryl's bat. The tiny girl took her place with an air of authority Will had never seen in her. Brittany was keenly aware of the fact that it was her direction which cost her the last batter, and she would pay.

She shook off the first signal from the catcher and nodded to the next. Will felt a mixed bag of emotions as his only child stood, uncharacteristically fearless, against a greater opponent. He feared for her failure, but felt so much pride in how she stared defiantly at the pitcher. He knew when she struck out he would, as a protective parent, want desperately to console her, but would be bound to his duties in the field. He dreaded watching her walk in dejection back to the dugout, dragging the unused bat behind her.

The fateful pitch was delivered, and Feryl laid her father's fears to rest with a powerful swing that sent the softball lobbing into the gap in right field. So transfixed was he that he failed to see Megan rounding third and racing for home. The young speedster had safely scored by the time Will saw his daughter slide into second base under the tag.

"Safe!" the umpire shouted, and Will screamed his exuberance. The bleachers cheered, and for that moment, for the first time in the history of Girls' 11 and Under softball, Feryl was the hero.

But that moment was past. Meghan Jordan stepped up to the plate. Will gave her one of the few signals they had and then looked to second base. To his astonishment, Feryl was giving him the "steal" signal. She wanted to go. He assessed the pitcher's stance and the catcher's foothold and then gave his frail, weak and sickly little girl the green light. His heart was in his throat as Brittany delivered the pitch.

Feryl left with the release and ran like none had ever seen her. The catcher came up and threw, but Feryl again slid under the baseman's mitt to the sound of "Safe!" The botched tag sent the loose ball rolling into the fence and out of play. The umpire made the call, and Will's daughter took the next base and her first run ever. Her teammates emptied the dugout to engulf her in cheers. Meagan Stanley, her hair wet and slimy from the conditioner, praised her, and even Rena managed a high five. Feryl was the happiest player in the world, and in a park filled with proud and doting parents, none among them was prouder than Will Billings.

The newfound skill and ability of his daughter and his team was the buzz of the league for the rest of that game, which was watched with great interest by a tall, sandy-haired man who never cheered or shouted but applauded whenever appropriate. He could not take his eyes off the coach and his ability to inspire others and instill confidence and even greatness by his mere presence and goodness. He had something that drew the best out of those around him. He could be special. He could even be the one. He could simply be a good coach, but there was clear potential in this man, he thought. There were many subtle phenomena occurring around the world that could attract the interest of someone such as this man, and many of them involved children or untainted humans, those open to the strange and unusual. He elected to look on but return to this man to see what he had.

That evening Feryl enjoyed her dinner much more than usual. Will relished in the seemingly healthy youth doing healthy youthful things. Playing ball. Eating her sandwich and dodging the vegetables. Talking with her mouth full. For this night and for this hour, she was normal. When the meal had been consumed and they had verbally relived her

22

triumph, Feryl stood to clear the table. Will stopped her and pointed to his watch.

"I'll get these, sweetie. You're way past due."

With her first expression of discontent, Feryl moped into her bedroom and left him to clean up. She was willing and even anxious to do the things a good daughter does. But some things were more important, and she knew her father would win the argument. Will watched her leave, ensuring she saw nothing of the heartbreak he suffered every time she was banished to her room.

Inside her room, Feryl walked to the shower, where she washed methodically with antiseptic soap and hypoallergenic shampoo. The last speck of softball field and all other potential contaminates ran down the check-drain, designed to close as soon as the water stopped. Her day washed away, Feryl exited the shower through the back door and sullenly retired to the confines of her sealed bedroom. The window allowed light, but no air. The door was closed and sealed and a clear plastic barrier kept her safe from the world outside.

The filtered intake fans were already blowing to clear the air of any remaining contaminants. Feryl swallowed several pills with bottled water. Some she took two at a time, but three of them were the size of horse tablets and had to taken individually. Once the last tablet was down, she sat on her bed and reached for her jewelry box.

She could not have seen her father come to the door and peer in. It still hurt him to see her in the protective bubble, but he took solace in the fact that she was able to take outings for greater periods now.

Watching her sit, almost grown to a normal teen, Will found himself reflecting on the years past, when his infant daughter had spent months in intensive care. It seemed a different lifetime ago when they had taken her in because of a routine infection. The baby had contracted an airborne virus. The chronic respiratory adenovirus was not usually so devastating, but in her weakened state, the bug embedded itself in her chest and lymph nodes and resisted antibiotics that could nearly kill its host.

As the child lived in a mechanical respirator for over a year, her mother and father bore the strain differently. The specialists urged Will and his wife to hope for the best, but mentally prepare themselves for the worst. Will remained steadfast, unwaveringly committed to her full recovery. But his wife Pamela was more accepting of the harsh hand dealt. She lashed out at the hospital and had malpractice lawyers on speed dial virtually from the initial diagnosis. She became cross with Will for refusing to admit the hospital had negligently killed their daughter. In her eyes and the eyes of her solicitors, his blind devotion to this lost cause was affecting the case and the settlement.

While Pamela was bent on compensation, Will was steadfast in his support of the hospital's efforts to help their child. Pamela had accepted the fact that their baby was lost, and the settlement was all that remained. She saw Will's determination as a threat to their case as it could only lessen the settlement, and the stress created a gap in their relationship that would not heal. Pamela could not be the supportive mother and partner the situation demanded, and Will would not excuse her from her duties. Nor would he join her campaign for compensation. They may have mortally injured her daughter, but *his* was alive and fighting. He would fight at her side with or without his wife. She chose the latter, and they separated before Feryl saw the outside of her mechanical respirator.

It would be another full year before Will was able to hold his daughter in his arms. She could breathe on her own, but her immune system was critically weak. Unable to recover from even the slightest cold or flu, she lived inside a sterile, plastic room specially designed to keep the air and surfaces germfree.

He spent virtually all of his time either with her or for her. When the divorce papers came, he hesitated only briefly. After signing for a clean break, he left Pamela to what she had and continued his work. Highly inventive, Will converted Feryl's bedroom to a self-contained safe room. The plastic environment was complete with three separate air filtration systems, two safe entrances and two back-up power supplies, one battery and one powered by a propane motor.

It had cost thousands beyond the hospital bills, half his business, and his marriage, but Will was proud to bring his baby home for her seventh birthday. With help from a loyal staff, he managed to keep his business running without sacrificing his single parent duties. Feryl was homeschooled by tutors and the Internet. He was fortunate to find a professional nurse who was a former schoolteacher, Matilda Brentfield. She was perfect for Feryl for two years.

When she was nine, Feryl's immune system had built up to a level able to defend her against most minor viruses, and it was suggested that she spend a few minutes a day outside the controlled environment. The monumental day she went into her living room and actually sat on the sofa with Will to watch television was a surreal pleasure for them both. It was so very sedate and normal that Will was moved to tears. They watched a situation comedy and laughed together like a normal family for the first time ever.

Each day she dared a little longer, ventured a bit further, tried a bit more than the day before. Will beamed with pride at the unshakable enthusiasm and courage the tiny child displayed. Small for her age and thin, her pallor added to the picture of a pitiably sick child. But she contradicted the image by her infectious smile and bubbly nature. Little could get her down for long, and she seemed to have accepted the foul hand life had dealt her with strength and dignity.

It was only in the past few months that her outings had become prolonged and increasingly energetic. To encourage this development, Will started the softball team so she could be among other girls doing normal girl things. She rarely participated to any degree, but was always present and positive. The team liked her and accepted her illness in stride. Only he still looked at her as frail or handicapped. As he watched her sitting on her bed, he almost dared think her well and normal.

Feryl opened the antique jewelry box. From the pink satin lining inside, a tiny ballerina stood on a spring and slowly turned to the tune of "Somewhere My Love."

"You should've seen it," she said into the box. "I got a hit and stole a base. I drove in a run and scored and everything. No, I didn't really steal it. That's just what they call it."

Will watched the imaginary conversation for a few moments before silently closing the door to respect her privacy.

As the door closed behind her, Feryl said into the box, "I know." She couldn't have known he was there or left, and yet she did. "Uh huh. I did that, too. Well, her hair was caught in the fence, and they couldn't get her... is that why I had it?" She giggled. "Oh yes, you do. Really?"

Feryl had developed a vivid imagination over her years of isolation. Often when she was alone, she would express thoughts or rehearse conversations aloud. Once able to venture outside, she kept such conversations to a minimum, though speaking her mind to no one in particular had become a trademark of hers. It was this trait which made it possible to hold these private conversations with Uriel without raising eyebrows. She had not always talked into her jewelry box, though Will had noticed it shortly after he gave it to her.

It was seven months earlier when Will found her weeping in her room. Peeking in, he saw her throwing moistened cotton balls at a framed portrait of her mother. She was clearly angry.

"We'll get by, honey."

"I know we will," she scowled. "We don't have a choice. Do we?"

Will was hesitant to misstep. "Do you... miss her?"

"No. I just wish she'd done it better. She ruined everything."

"By leaving? Sweetie, you were too little to remember what it was like when she was here. She pretty much ruined everything by staying."

"I know. I remember when I was at St Helen's."

"You were miserable."

"So were you."

"I could put up with her if it was just me."

"You're like that though. You never get mad at people. You're like that Gandy guy."

"Gandy? You mean Gandhi? Mahatma Gandhi?"

"Yeah. That little bald guy in the diaper. You're almost him, but with more hair and clothes."

"Well, that's a bit of an overstatement. But the point is that you're the one who told her to leave."

"I know!" She threw another cotton ball with greater force.

"So now you're sad about it?"

"Not about that. But she was supposed to do a lot of things that you don't."

"Like what?"

"Like get me girl stuff. I don't have a training bra. I'll never get a thong if I have to wait for you."

"I didn't know you needed one. And probably true."

"And I don't have any jewelry. Nothing. You can't even let me get my ears pierced. I hate to think what'll happen when I get my period."

The comment was enough to turn Will out of the room. But he managed to stop himself and pull up the only chair outside her protective plastic. Sitting down as close to her as he could, he almost dared a smile. "So dealing with the here and now, please, if you did have jewelry, where would you keep it?"

"On me. I'd wear it all. All the time."

"Seriously."

"Grandma does it."

"Grandma's a hundred."

"So?"

"So she also thinks Bing Crosby lives under her bed, and I happen to know she doesn't sleep in her jewelry."

"Okay, so I don't have a jewelry box either. One more thing to add to the 'I hate her' list."

Will reached out into the hall and produced a package wrapped in festive birthday gift paper. "Here's a start." He slid the box into the trap drawer designed to allow passage. "It's okay. It's clean."

Feryl beamed with delight as she tore open the present,

an ornate, antique jewelry box. She had only a vague concept of how hard it had been for Will to restore and completely decontaminate the box. As she opened it, a tiny ballerina stood on her spring mount and began to turn to the plinking music box. Feryl didn't know what the song was, but it was pretty. It was something a mother, a good mother, might give her little girl.

Inside the box, she saw a velvet-covered earring tray. She lifted it out and found a bracelet and matching necklace in the bottom. She had jewelry. It was childish and clearly inexpensive looking, but it was hers.

"It's just a start," Will said. "The more you get out and about, the faster you'll fill it with precious gems and stones. It'll be a treasure chest in no time."

"Yeah, right."

"You're welcome."

"Sorry, Daddy. I really love it. I know I'll get stuff for it."

"Well, after my interview tomorrow, we may be able to fill it a bit faster."

"Are you going to be on TV?"

"I think so. They're just filming it tomorrow, but they sounded pretty interested in the wheelchair. If they air it, I'll use it to promote the rest of the shop, and we should take off."

"What did you tell me about shoulds and shouldn'ts?"

"I know. But sometimes it's all you have. Wish me luck."

"Luck."

"Now get some sleep."

"'Kay. Love you."

"You, too, sweetie. G'night."

Feryl had gone to bed that night, but did nothing resembling sleep. She had for most of her life found benefit in the ability to entertain herself. She had always been her own best friend and trusted herself implicitly. It was in the wee hours of the night that she was most prone to let her imagination run free. That night she studied her new treasure chest so devoid of treasure. She believed her father that it would someday be brimming with precious stones, but she could not wait. Something had to go into the box now. She peered out the window at the flickering lights. Lightning bugs danced around her backyard. Tiny gem flies daring her. The temptation was too great.

In her jammies and tennis shoes, Feryl silently slipped out of her plastic world and outside. As protective as he had always been, Will never felt the need to watch her at night. Feryl had almost never misbehaved and could easily open the double doors to her protective room without his help.

Behind the house, the chain link fenced-in yard had very few toys or things of a healthy growing child. Beyond the four-foot tall fence was an overgrown wooded area. The night air was cool, but nowhere near cold. She made her way by moonlight across the back yard and snared her first, then a second, firefly and placed it in the box. The lightning bugs seemed to sense her intent and vanished into the trees. She had not gathered nearly enough treasure to be content and continued into the wooded field behind her house.

Even through the trees, the moonlight guided her in search of anything shiny. She found a few smooth stones and a bottle cap. As she turned, something on the ground flickered. She moved toward the sparkle and found it at the base of one of the larger, older trees in the tiny woods. It was a shard of deep blue glass. It was about the size of an infant's hand and curved as if from a broken bottle. But the edges were smoothed, possibly with age. It was old, but beautiful. Clean and shiny, the glass treasure was destined for her box.

Feryl suddenly felt an odd sensation, like someone was watching her, but more pronounced, yet much more foreign. It was as if she heard someone, but no sound was made. She looked around cautiously. No one was near. But again, even as she looked for it, she heard, no, sensed she was being watched. She looked down at the glass.

"I'm not stealing. I just found it," she said as if in response to the unasked question.

Again the thoughts came to her, as if implanted in her mind, and she heard a voice speaking. It was tiny, faint at first. But the words and mood were as clear as day.

"Humans think anything that doesn't have a name on it is theirs. Please put it back and go."

"Who... is that?" Feryl asked of the air around her. "Who's talking?" Too fearful to wait for a response, she complied with the demand and bent to put the glass back. As she leaned, she inadvertently glanced through the glass. Through the blue tint, she clearly saw her host sitting in the sparse grass at the base of the tree.

The tiny person was a wispy girl, thin and white and barely four inches tall, more than two of that made up by legs. At first glance her body appeared featureless and naked. But as Feryl adjusted the glass lens, she saw the tiny girl wearing a sheer garment. She had long, incredibly fine honey blonde hair and was very pretty despite her angry scowl. On her back and nearly the size of her again was a pair of elegant silver-white wings. The moth-like wings were almost transparent and as delicate as a layer of frost on a spider's web. She glared at Feryl with large green eyes.

"I am speaking, Feryl. Now kindly drop my crystal and go." Feryl sensed the words as though they were whispered to her, but the tiny lips did not move. It was like distinctly remembering a voice and words only just spoken.

Still gasping at the magical image, Feryl tried to still her ire. "I'm terribly sorry. Here." She went to return the shard and realized that she could no longer see the fairy. She held the glass up again and saw her still staring angrily back. "I can't see you. May I borrow it just for a minute? Just to talk?"

The fairy looked side to side as if fearful someone might see her soften her mood. Then she looked up at the giant. "Will you promise to leave it when you go?"

"I swear. You can trust me."

"I know. I rarely see humans worthy of any trust at all. And it is much easier to speak to you if we can look at each other."

"So you've spoken to others?"

"Oh yes. But I never know how it will go. The last fellow couldn't see me and went running through the woods screaming that he was possessed."

Feryl laughed and was pleased to see the fairy giggling as well. She was human enough to talk to. "So how do you know who to trust?"

"Your aura is very clear. I love the color, too."

"My aura?"

"It's an energy field that surrounds all living things. It changes with your mood and thought. If you lied or even thought about telling a lie, it would turn an ugly gray. If you're angry, it's red or purple. Mean people with no compassion have a pale yellow aura."

"Like mustard?"

"Mustard?"

"Yeah. You know. Like..." Feryl mimed the act of spreading mustard on a hot dog.

"I know what it is. Do I look like I eat hot dogs, Feryl?"

"No. You look like a hot dog could eat you. Sorry." She giggled.

The fairy was neither insulted nor amused. "There are as many shades and intensities of auras as there are emotions to be felt. I like yours."

"Does that mean you like me?"

"Not yet. Give it time, Feryl."

"And that's another thing. How do you know my name? Is that in the aura thing, too?"

"Another time. Your aura just changed. Do you feel all right?"

"I have to go back to my room pretty soon, or I'll get sick. Will you be here tomorrow?"

"Wait. Let me see your hand. Bring it close."

Still holding the glass to her eye with her right hand, Feryl extended her left with no fear or trepidation. The fairy leaned over her palm and looked at the lines. She examined the child's frail fingers and even the nails. "All right. Leave my crystal and go home. I'll be here tomorrow."

Feryl did leave for the security of her oxygen tent. The extra outing and fatigue left her weakened, so she spent the next two days inside the tent on increased meds. But she returned to the tree on the third night and for several afterward. They spent hours talking about anything Feryl could think of. Uriel, as the fairy eventually introduced herself, had a seemingly insatiable curiosity about Feryl's life and family and about humans in general. They talked about her illness only during the first week or two, and it was never mentioned again. Each time Feryl came out to see her, they seemed to have an entirely new conversation.

Feryl lay on the grass and looked through the glass shard as she had most every night after dinner. "Do you have boys and girls?"

"Do I look like a girl?" Uriel asked.

"You look like a pretty girl. Like a model."

"Some of us look like boys. but not like humans. We pick our body mostly to talk to you. We don't need them."

"So you don't have a mom and dad?"

"I used to feel sad about that. No. We were always here. We don't have families like you do. Sometimes that is good, but some of you don't appreciate how lucky you are to have someone so close to you."

"I suppose that's because some of us have relatives that aren't very nice."

"What about boyfriends?"

Feryl failed to restrain her childish embarrassment. "What about them?"

"Do you have a boyfriend?"

"What? Like have I kissed a boy, you mean?"

"I didn't mean that, but I was going to ask that."

"Well no and not yet, but I think about it."

"All girls do."

"How do you know?"

"You're not the first person I've spoken with. I love learning about what it's like to have a real body and the emotions that go with it. You have so many strengths and weaknesses." You're all so very different."

"That's me all right. Different."

"You're very special, Feryl."

"Yeah. That's why my only friends are on the internet when Dad lets me on line or in books. I'll probably never kiss a boy."

"Do you want to?"

Feryl smiled coyly. "Maybe."

"Promise to tell me when you do. I'd love to hear what it feels like. Tell me while it's still fresh."

"Kay."

Feryl was homeschooled and had only interacted with actual classrooms online. Her improving health and strength had not gone unnoticed by her protective father. One evening Feryl seemed to wolf her dinner down as she had never done before.

"Whoa. Slow down, Tiger," Will cautioned her. "What's the rush?"

"Nothing. I'm just hungry."

"Well, I have to admit my recipe is unmatched. The secret it to preheat the oven before putting the fish sticks in."

"Shut up. Can I go out and play for a while?"

"Don't see why not. Know what else I'm thinking?"

"That I need to start doing the dishes?"

"Soon. But I was thinking that if you keep getting better, I thought I might... You know... If you want to..."

"What, Daddy?"

"I thought I might enroll you in school. If you're ready, I mean."

Feryl lit up. "School? Real school? With teachers and homework and other people?"

"Not just yet. But maybe next semester if Doctor Drake says it's okay. What do you think?"

Feryl leapt out of her chair and rounded the table to throw her arms around her father. "What do you think I think? Thank you, Daddy. Now can I go out? Just for a bit?"

"Okay, Bud. Just for an hour. We don't want to mess this up."

Feryl ran through the woods as fast as she could. She was bursting to share the news with her best friend. When she got to the tree and lifted the shard, she watched Uriel seemingly wake from a sound nap.

"Wake up, sleepy head. Guess what?"

Uriel rolled over and sat up in the grass. "Sorry. I'm just tired lately. What happened?"

"I get to go to school! Not yet but pretty soon. Know what that means? Other people. Maybe boys. What do you think of that?"

"That's wonderful news, Feryl. I'm very happy for you." She smiled as best she could, but her oversized eyes slowly closed as though she was falling back to sleep.

Feryl had noticed over the past week or so that her tiny friend was growing increasingly lethargic, but as they mostly sat and talked with a minimum of activity, Uriel's moving less only now seemed important.

"Are you alright?"

"Odd question. I don't think I've ever been asked that."

"But you know everything. You know what's wrong?"

"I only know my time is running out."

"Running out? What does that mean? You live forever. You said so."

"We don't live. Not like you. And nothing is forever. Don't worry. We have time. I just need to rest. That's all." She lay down again and started to close her eyes.

"I know that look," Feryl said. "You're getting sick. Am I doing it?"

"No. It's just happening. It's the air. The more I breathe, the weaker I become. Perhaps I'll stop breathing."

"No!" Feryl shouted. "I know what to do."

She ran back to her room and returned with the jewelry box. Uriel was too weak to object, and she and her crystal were placed inside. Feryl took them to her sterile, protected world so the fairy could be safe from the poisoned air which threatened them both. Neither she nor her new houseguest ever doubted her intent.

In the clean air and protected environment, Feryl watched as Uriel began to regain her strength. Feryl proved to be the world's first fairy doctor, and her payment was an on-site, full-time friend. She loved the immediacy of their friendship, the way she could talk to Uriel any time she wanted and how Uriel spoke to her when she didn't want to be disturbed. She could hear the fairy's words when she was on the phone or washing or trying on clothes.

Her father's revelation about school was a perfect excuse

for her spending so much more time at home. She told Will she did not want to risk getting sick and not being allowed to enroll so she would not need to play in the woods for a while.

Uriel influenced her dress and manner, and Feryl was becoming noticeably more flamboyant and outgoing. Many, including her doctors, noticed that she was getting stronger and healthier at an unprecedented rate. It was more than a positive energy drawn from Uriel. The combination of their energies seemed beneficial to them both. Uriel was again able to fly after a few short weeks in the purified air. Her incredibly delicate wings seemed too frail to touch or even move, but the pure energy welling in Uriel bound together the glistening particles that made up her wings. So broad were her wings that the slightest flutter easily lifted the virtually weightless fairy into the air. She spent much of her time flitting about the brightly-colored bedroom, especially near the electrical outlets and appliances.

The friendship flourished, and every day Feryl seemed to have a bit more to share with her best friend. This day it was the home run and her good deed. She told Uriel how proud her father was of her, and Uriel knew from her aura how important that was to her.

The Fifth Chapter

Karen was left with no alternative but to go home for the evening. Thanks to Vic, she got flagged every time she logged onto the Internet or sent an E-mail. He had deliberately made it impossible for her to get anything done at the office. She wanted only to find a way to feel needed at work, but after an afternoon wasted, Karen was forced to concede and took herself out of the workplace and to the last place she wanted to be.

She had spent so few evenings free or at home, and those few were generally spent catching up on email or compiling data for her next step. With no next step in sight, she was feeling somewhat lost.

She walked into the spacious apartment. It was sparsely decorated and slightly disorganized. There were always more important things to do than laundry or dusting. Now there was nothing keeping her from the menial chores other than a profound lack of desire. She walked aimlessly through the apartment, dropping garments along the way from the door to the kitchen. Her stylish shoes, her business suit coat, the tailored skirt and even the now restrictive and unnecessary pantyhose were left on the floor. The smart, partially unbuttoned unisex shirt was covering enough, and she tapped the answering machine on the way past.

"Karen? Hi. This is Eddie Marks. We met at the Blain function last week? I said I might give you a call if I was in town so…"

She tapped to bypass Eddie Marks. "Loser," she muttered. "Time, time everywhere but nary a second for you." The machine beeped and continued to the next message as she left it to run and moved into the kitchen. She wasn't hungry. She simply had nowhere else to go.

"*Miss* Gabriel? This is the Aubrey Street Shell. Your car is ready. You can pick it up any time. Thank you." Beep.

"*Hello*? Is this…? Sorry. I must have misdialed." Beep.

"Karen? Vic. Your flight is moved to two-forty on

Friday. I'll send a car around to get you and your bags. Don't give the driver a hard time." Beep.

She emerged with a bottle of water and looked at the machine. No more new messages. Another first. She pressed the "delete" button on the machine and nearly knocked over the glass snowball next to it. She picked up the ornament and gave it a shake. The glistening white flakes were meant to swirl around the tiny Empire State Building and cityscape. She noticed the flakes falling oddly to the bottom with no hesitation. She shook the dome more vigorously, but the flakes seemed to refuse to do anything other than fall listlessly to the bottom.

"Story of my life," she mumbled as she set the dome back on the table and went to take a bath. She spent as long as she could stand in the tranquil tub. Normally a hit-and-run shower person, she was doing her best to adapt to idle time. She put on a pair of sweat pants and a New Orleans Saints T-shirt and packed for her trip.

Messages checked, bath taken, dinner eaten, suitcase packed, and it was only seven-thirty. She sat on her plush sofa for what may have been only the third time in six months. The television remote was within reach so she elected to channel surf for a while. Sitcoms, television dramas and two reality shows failed to stay her thumb from machine-gunning through the stations. She stopped when an announcer used the word alternate fuel. The program, just ending, had apparently been devoted to the search for alternatives to fossil fuels.

She had already set the remote down when the program ended and could not muster the energy to pick it up again. So she braved the obligatory commercials that led to the next news capsule program.

"Hello and welcome to *Hidden Genius*, the show that searches for the real brains in the world. I'm Harry Boswick. We've all heard the success stories of the secretary who invented typing correction fluid or the music teacher who invented Post-Its. True or not, we've all had at least one idea, great or small, that we knew would be a huge moneymaker if we could just get it out there. Tonight our roving investigator, David Mercado, has uncovered what may be the last true independent inventor. Get ready to be amazed at the truly revolutionary products you're about to see. This is the only place most of them can be found."

The scene changed to the front door of a shop called *I Wish I'd Thought of That!* The young reporter donned a professional smile as the camera came in on him. "Ever have trouble holding a potato while you try to peel it? If your hands seem to get in the way you might want one of these." He held up a plastic pistol-shaped object with a potato held firmly between the points where a barrel would be. As he repeatedly squeezed the trigger, the potato, gripped only at the ends like a tiny lathe, was slowly rotated. "With this Spud-Wrench, I can easily peel the potato without losing my grip or slicing my fingers. The only place you can get one of these is from this very aptly named store. If you've been looking for something you can't seem to find anywhere but you're sure it should exist, stay with me."

He entered the shop, where the nervously grinning owner greeted him. "This is Will Billings, store owner, entrepreneur and, dare I say it, brilliant inventor. Will? How did you start as an inventor?"

Will cleared his throat and tried not to stare at the camera as he replied. "Well, it started when I came up with an idea, as we all do, about something that should exist and thought somebody should make that."

"What was that? Do you remember?"

"I think it was the shower scrubbers. A normal pair of thongs with scrubby bottoms. You could wear them in the shower and clean the tub while you make it dirty."

"Just by walking around. Seems like a good idea."

"Uh huh. So I thought, why don't we have that?" So I decided to give it a try. One thing led to another and..." He gestured grandly toward the store.

"We've seen the Spud-Wrench. Can you show us a few more of your patented products?"

"Love to, David," Will said, as he raised a plastic handle with two opposing flyswatter-like paddles on the end. With a squeeze of the trigger the paddles slapped together with a 'pop.' "This is something I call the fly-whapper. You know how you have to wait for a fly to land and then sneak up on it with a conventional flyswatter?"

"Sometimes I think they know it."

"Well with this, you can swat them right out of the air. Just aim and squeeze." POP! "I've got a modified version with edges that overlap."

"What's that for?"

"It's a humane spider trap. For those people who don't want to kill the spiders but hate picking them up, you just scoop them up and take them outside."

"Brilliant. And you own the patent on this?"

"Like most of the things in here. This is another version of that with a different application." He held up what appeared to be a back-scratcher with a slightly heavier handle. He bent the flexible shaft so it fit over his shoulder, and he easily reached the middle of his back.

"That's convenient," David commented.

"Watch. It gets better." Will turned around so the camera could see the tiny scratching hand. As Will squeezed the handle, the hand opened and closed like a real hand to effectively scratch the most awkward part of his back. He put the gadget down and moved on with the guided tour. "Look at these." He directed the camera to a display rack of what appeared to be tiny disguises. As he held one up to show the back, it was clearly a child's pacifier. It was different as the front was a large pair of red lips.

"What's this? Costumes for babies?"

"Not really, David. See I just got tired of seeing that stupid ring hanging out of the mouth of every baby I saw. It was like we took them home and hung them in the closet. I decided to have some fun with my daughter and came up with this one. The back is a conventional pacifier, but the front is a little more personal."

He placed the pacifier into the mouth of a life-size doll head next to the display rack. The baby instantly had a big, red pucker. There were three doll heads there, and he produced two more designs. One was a tiny mustache, beard and pipe. The other was a mouth blowing bubbles. The rack showed a disgusting set of crooked "Billy-Bob" teeth chewing on a plastic bug, a set of vampire fangs dripping with crimson blood, a hobo mouth with stubble and a short cigar, a mouth with extended tongue and even a plastic coach's whistle that really worked.

"These are brilliant," David said. "What else is there?"

"Well," Will pondered as he glanced behind him. "Ever drop a phone in the middle of a conversation?"

"Of course."

Will picked up a cordless handset and put it to his ear. "Or sometimes you just get bad news and have to just..." In a mock display of temper, Will threw the phone to the floor. To the reporter's amazement, the phone bounced back into Will's hand seemingly unscathed.

"Is that a real phone?" David asked.

"As real as any. The wires and components are normal. But the case is foam rubber. You can drop it, throw it or let the baby chew on it, and it bounces right back. I call it Fone Rubber."

Will easily filled the twenty-two minute segment with a broad variety of products. He had a cloth tube which was open on both ends. If you pulled a coiled wire or cable through it, the wire never got tangled. It was perfect for Christmas lights or electric cords. He had pool gadgets like disposable pool shoes that could be dispensed from a vending machine and swim fins which strapped to the side of a swimmer's ankles and flopped in and out as the swimmer stepped. Acting like an underwater stair climber, the fins made it possible to tread water effortlessly for hours.

Most of the inventions were small and inexpensive novelty items. The shopping blinders were little more than a gag gift, but few men walked past them without noticing. The blinders were set on a plastic head band that sported two fabric covered squares on the sides. When worn correctly by a woman, the blinders shielded her peripheral vision to guard against impulse shopping. She could only see straight ahead. Despite the obvious sexist connotations it had proven a very popular stocking stuffer. He had a cache of small and large items that he raced through for the camera, deliberately saving his favorite for last.

Picking up what appeared to be a life-sized pair of gorilla arms, Will slipped his hands into them.

"Another toy?" David guessed.

"Not really. These are real crutches. I noticed a boy trying to shop with his arms in little crutches, and I got the idea that it should be more fun for the kid." As he spoke, he walked through the store like a talking ape on the floor-length, hairy arms. The rubberized knuckles held the floor well though only a small point in the center actually touched. "I've got ape, Hulk and Thing arms that cover any conventional aluminum crutch."

"It looks like for fun, but how does it help him shop or get through life?"

"You mean other than looking cool?" Will lifted the arm toward a packaged figurine on the shelf, and to David's astonishment the rubber fist opened and grasped the package. Will lifted the plastic bag and set it on the counter with the gigantic hand and extended reach.

"I've also got bat and bird wings, but they don't have hands. They just look cool. Even kids that don't need them will want them," he said as he ape-walked with David to a wheelchair in the back of the shop. He set the crutches down as he pointed to the chair. "This one is something I just recently came up with."

"I saw this, but I didn't want to say anything."

"I know. It's always a sensitive subject, and I think a lot of opportunities are missed because we're afraid of offending someone. But I was in a grocery store once, and a person asked me to get something off the top shelf for her. I wondered what she'd have done if I hadn't been there."

"Settled for generic, probably."

"Well, she doesn't have to settle anymore." Will sat in the chair and turned it on. "I have a friend who works in robotics. He built this thing for me and I wired it to the chair. Watch this." Using fingertip controls, he maneuvered the chair through the store to a shelf higher than David's eye level. At a touch of the control pad on the arm of the chair, Will was able to raise and extend a mechanical arm from the side of the chair. It reached up and out and grasped a bag of toys from the top shelf. With unexpected ease, Will brought the bag down and gently placed it in the basket attached to the side of the chair.

"You want freedom? I could reach anything you can with one finger."

"This is amazing. And you own the patent on all of this?"

"Most of it. I have a few inventor friends who bring things in from time to time. That cable sock belongs to my brother-in-law. I just sell it for him."

"So you at least will someday profit from all of your ideas."

"One way or another, I guess. Sometimes I trade or just give it up."

"You give your ideas away?"

"Or trade. See the guy who built this robot arm, for example, didn't want to work for free, and I couldn't afford a robotics engineer. So I gave him a different idea in exchange for this one."

"Are you allowed to share it?"

"Well. Have you seen the Honda robot which can negotiate stairs? Major milestone in technology." As he spoke, Will pulled a rolled up stack of diagrams from behind the counter and unfurled them for the camera and David. "I just happen to have these handy. See that program got me thinking. The only reason it looks human is for acceptance. I designed one with the same technology but with flat legs and no head or arms. A paraplegic could strap this device onto his own legs and mechanically walk instead of trundle. He couldn't run. At least not yet. But he could stand and walk. What would that be worth?"

"He'd be kind of like Robocop. Wouldn't he? All mechanical and stuff?"

"A bit. But a physical therapist I know thought it would be excellent conditioning for the muscles. I just thought it would be a good application for the technology."

"Where would the control pad go?"

"Depends. It could be hand-held like a game controller. But I'm watching this new technology where a rat's brain is operating a robot motor. That could be the future here. Strap a robotic shell to your legs. Put on the controller cap and walk away happy. Cool, huh?"

"Light years beyond cool." David turned to the camera. "Well, there it is. One of the best 'Local boys makes good' stories I've ever covered. Will, thank you for having us and good luck with... all of this. Back to you, Harry."

The scene switched back to a smiling Harry Boswick. "Thank you, David. That's one inventor who's sure to do well. And now a different kind of success story: here's one about a mallard that plays soccer. And he's good."

*****

Pamela Billings-Trudeau sat and fumed at the story of her ex-husband doing better than he had during their marriage. With the television muted to avoid distracting her from her thoughts, she stared in annoyance as her present husband walked into the bedroom and prepared to get into bed.

"Tell me you didn't leave all of your dirty clothes all over the bathroom," she barked at him.

Everett stopped before his second leg left the floor. "They're in the laundry basket."

"So we just leave piles of clothes lying around? Is that how we live?"

"Well, you got rid of the hamper. What do you—"

"Because you kept leaving it full of dirty clothes."

"But that's what it's for."

"It was an excuse for you to be messier. God help us if anyone actually dropped by. If they looked in there and your dirty undies were thrown around..."

Everett was already out of bed and returning to the bathroom without bothering to ask her who would drop in to their home unannounced, go upstairs to peek in the laundry basket and then judge them for having laundry in it (or why they would have such friends). Knowing it was only prolonging the inevitable, he gathered the clothes and took them to the laundry room. No hamper or basket was to be found, so he put them into the washing machine. He took two steps before stopping himself. He knew what her next question would be, and he prepared his response by starting the washer. He could do no more.

When he returned to the bedroom, she was still talking. "It's bad enough the sink is always full of dishes. And what did you do with them? Leave them on the floor in the laundry room?"

"In the washer." He spoke in an exhausted monotone as he attempted to get to bed.

"Just lying there?"

"I started it."

"So the dirty t-shirt you're wearing can just lie around for another week. Is that it?"

Already beaten into submission, he climbed out of bed without argument and headed back toward the laundry, removing his shirt in stride.

He returned to the bedroom naked and truly believed she would have no response. He was again mistaken.

"Can you set the alarm for ninety minutes?"

"Why?"

"Well, somebody has to put that load in the dryer. Or did you plan to just let it lay there and get all musty? That's where mildew comes from."

Everett hesitated for a moment. His defeat absolute, he stood and left the room. He stayed up until every garment he owned was washed, dried, ironed and put away. Even at this point, he walked cautiously back to bed. The soft snoring sound told him Pamela was fast asleep, and he did his best to slip into bed without stirring her. He hoped everything was done that could be done, but he would not underestimate her again.

"Goodnight, Sweetheart," he whispered.

"Goodnight, Love," she answered softly. "Thank you."

Everett allowed a subtle smile before drifting off to sleep.

The Sixth Chapter

Friday came and eleven o'clock arrived with a text message to Karen that her driver was outside. She had spent a day and a half dreading what should be a relaxing vacation in a beautiful resort. She could not seem to let go of the nagging suspicion that something was wrong. Something was so very different about what she should have felt upon the completion of her project that it felt incomplete. This was something she should not have been able to deal with. It should have made her crazy. But this was less disturbing to her than the welling sense of euphoric disconnection. She felt as though she could drift off into a trance or even a coma if she allowed herself. What was that? Why did she not care more? What had they done to her?

The chiming of the doorbell brought her again to reality, a state she had been finding it increasingly difficult to hold on to. She opened the door and the driver smiled.

"International airport?"

"Do I have a choice?" she said as she turned to point to her bags.

The driver chuckled. "Yeah. I guess you could not go. Last I checked we were still in America." He stepped in and reached for the largest suitcase.

The comment seemed to stick with her. "Yeah. There's an option." She tapped him on the shoulder. "I didn't get your name."

He looked up and smiled. "Bob."

"Bob?"

"Yes Ma'am."

"Get out, Bob."

The stunned driver was escorted out into the corridor. As the door closed behind him, Bob was left with nothing to do but smell his underarms to try to determine the cause of his rejection. After a moment to insure she was serious, he spoke to the door. "I'll just head back then. Okay?" A twenty dollar tip slid under the door to convince him his work was done. Accepting the tip, Bob returned to the car and drove away.

Inside, Karen mentally reran the events of the past few minutes. "Odd decision," she thought. She could only hope she would be able to come up with something to justify her presence to the office and to justify missing a paid vacation to herself.

*****

It was Saturday and no softball game was scheduled. Feryl took advantage of the time she was allowed to spend outside her protected environment and dove into a project she had been developing in her mind for weeks.

Will was at the store, and her sitter was watching television, so she had unsupervised freedom to delve into Will's workshop. The garage had been converted into an elaborate and versatile workshop. He had walls devoted to woodworking, metal, electrical and technical projects. The table in the center of the room was where Feryl had set up assembly of her special project. She had a glass dome and a faux silver turkey platter. The two were to be combined to create a self-enclosed biosphere. Her plan was to somehow seal them together with some potted plants and moss. It would be a tiny woodland paradise. All she had to do was find a way to bind the top and bottom together, and the rest would be simple.

Bits and pieces from Will's many projects littered the work surface, and she tried to put them in their place as she worked. Some of the junk included a golf grip, which she slid onto the end of a pool cue merely because it seemed to fit, and a pen light laser, which she played with for a few seconds before setting it aside. It was fun, but she had work to do.

Will had come home to find the sitter in the kitchen doing dishes. "Hey, Danielle. Are you still in high school?"

"I graduated last year. Why?"

"You took French. Right?"

"I got an A."

46

"Perfect. Watch this." Will excitedly held a small digital voice recorder to his mouth and spoke into the mic. "How much did you pay for that shirt?" He quickly held up a finger to stay her from responding while he pressed a playback button on his recorder. To Danielle's amazement it repeated his question in French. He held his hand up to keep her from replying until he had reversed the buttons and pressed record. Then he lowered his hand and mouthed to her "In French."

Danielle replied to him in French as best she could remember from high school. Will made sure she was finished, and then he pressed the playback button. A digital voice came from the recorder speaking in English.

"I don't know. It is my mother's."

"Oh my God," Danielle exclaimed. "A digital translator. How cool."

"Uh huh. They already had the voice to text and vice versa program. In fact most of it already existed. I had a geek I know link the programs and merge them onto this thing and voila! Think how many of these babies I could sell at international airports. In French, Spanish, Italian. And we could offer additional language downloads like Polish or Lithuanian."

"You could like sell it to Motorola for a phone feature. That is so cool. Can I have that one?"

"No. Where's our girl?"

"Playing in the shop. She said you said it was all right."

Will grimaced. "Actually, Danielle, I'd rather she not go out there without supervision. Tools and chemicals, you know."

"Oh sorry. I've pretty much learned to trust her. She's not like most kids her age."

"Very true. It's okay. I'll get her."

He stepped softly out to the back of the house. He stood and listened as Feryl sang as she worked. It initially sounded like she was singing *Guantanamara* and even had a poor Hispanic accent. As was her way, the tune was familiar, but the words were totally her own.

"One scary meadow! Well this is one scary meadow.

One scary meaaaaaa... dow. Well ain't this one scary mea...dow."

He snickered at the improvisation. "What's that? Bambi's mother's theme?" he asked as he entered the shop.

Feryl turned long enough to extend a smile of greeting before returning to her work. "Hi, Daddy. You're early."

"Slow day. Glen can handle it. If your project is half as inventive as your lyrics, I'll make a fortune on it."

"It's just a thing."

"For school?"

"Um. Sure. It's a school project. So you can't help me."

"Okay."

"Unless I ask."

"Sounds fair."

"So how can I put a door in this and keep it air-tight?"

"Well, that didn't take long." Will smiled and dove in to help Feryl with the project. It was elementary for him, so he merely lent guidance when she needed it. She did the bulk herself until he insisted she break for dinner.

The next day saw her biosphere unfinished and unattended as she was due for her regular doctor's visit. The barrage of blood tests, breath measures and questions had become so routine to her that her doctor never bothered to ask. He simply asked her to assume the position on the table, and she began spewing the answers.

"No, I haven't noticed any bleeding or shortness of breath. My temperature and appetite are normal. I can see fine and nothing hurts except for the toe I stubbed, and yes I said a bad word when I did it and I'm sorry."

"So when did you change from my favorite patient to my biggest little pain?"

"Last time you..." she cringed as he pierced her arm with the large needle. "...tried to kill me."

Will had long ago been banished from the examination room. His questions had become so redundant that even Feryl was answering them and telling him he should know by now. He still fidgeted nervously the entire time she was inside. And she emerged each time with a broad smile, a brightly colored bandage on her arm and a lollipop.

That night they had their usual supper and a movie before she was again sent to the security of the oxygen tent. The next morning, she was anxious to get out into the open air. Will forced her to stay in until breakfast was ready, and she could come out with the promise of returning immediately after. She hated it, having had a greater taste of normality, but she knew her father was right. Her body was gaining resistance to the environment, but it was still possible to push too hard. During breakfast, she persuaded him to extend her leave for a walk to the store and back.

Will was doing the dishes and watching the road through the window when the phone rang. When he heard Feryl's doctor's voice, he felt a surge of dread.

"What's wrong, Doctor?"

"Nothing," was the response. His tone was flippant to the point of mockery.

"Nothing?"

"Not a thing."

"So why are you scaring me on a Sunday?"

"When was the last time I ran all the tests on Feryl and said that nothing was wrong?"

Will took his tone and thought. "What's up, Drake?"

"It's the damnedest thing. I know she's been doing really good lately. But this time we found nothing. I mean zip. It was as if she was never sick."

"Are you serious?"

"Will, her immune system is stronger than yours. Her lymphs are clear, and her lung capacity is perfect. She's beaten it. She's finally beaten the virus. There's absolutely no trace of it in her at all."

Will was stunned. "So what do we do now?"

"Well, I'm screwed. I just made a down payment on a new boat. Since I don't need to see her again like... ever... I'll have to cut back."

"Drake. You've been a part of our lives since she was a baby, and you're a good friend, but I'm still waiting for the doctor part to kick in. Where's the down side?"

"I'll keep an eye on her for a while just to be sure. But there's no second shoe to drop. As your doctor and your friend, I'm delighted to tell you to have a good life, Will. You've got a normal kid at last."

Will put the phone down and stared at the window as if hypnotized. He went into her room and looked at the plastic sterile prison that had been her home for most of her life. No more. Then he finally dared let it sink in. After years of wishing it had never happened, of praying for her and trying to be upbeat and positive for her sake, he could finally and at long last relax. He was not sure he knew how, but it came in a single burst as he suddenly howled at the ceiling.

Feryl had found most of what she needed plus another trinket for her jewelry box at the mall. She strolled casually home with her bags and hopes and announced her presence as she entered the house.

"Helloooooo? Anybody home? Poor little sick child all alone here!"

"In here, Feryl!" Will called from her bedroom. "Get ready for a surprise."

She hurried into the room expecting something between a television and a pony. What she found was on a totally different line. Her room had been completely gutted. Every protective plastic wall and covering was torn off and thrown out the open window. Fresh air wafted through her once sterile environment. But for the naked screws and nail holes, it was a normal room.

"What did you do?"

"Something I've been wanting to do since you were a baby."

"But… can I do this?"

"Your doctor gave you a clean bill of health. You're well."

She finally started to get it. Like her father, she had spent years imagining this moment, but she never dared dream it would actually happen. Her smile reached nearly ear to ear as she gazed about the normality. The normal bed. The normal window. The normal … jewelry box. Her heart dropped.

"Daddy! Put it back!"

"What? No, honey. You don't need it anymore."

"It's working, so they want me to stop using it? Does that make sense to you?"

"Yes. Your doctor said you have to let your body learn to heal itself."

"I can't. Not yet! Fix it! Hurry, Daddy. Please!" She was between pleading and panic as she clung to her father's shirt. "You don't understand!"

Will bent near her and held her by both arms. "Feryl. It's not just that you can do without the tent. You need to. Your body is working now, and if you don't let it, you'll get weaker and start getting sick again. You have to let it learn to heal itself. Do you understand? You can do this. You have to."

She made no attempt to stop the tears. "Daddy. Listen. Do I want to be out and be normal?"

"What?"

"Do I? Have you ever heard me ask?"

"Of course. We've been talking about it forever."

"And do I ever tell lies to you? Ever?"

Will was beginning to sense a bigger problem. "No, sweetie. Never. What's wrong?"

"I need you to trust me, Daddy. It's really, really super important. Can you not think or be a dad and just do something extra huge just because I really need you to?"

As much as he had always hoped to be a friend to her, Will found the request to turn off the dad function extremely difficult. "Honey. I can't let you live in that room again. Not if it could hurt you or make you sick again. You can hate me if you want. But you'll be healthy when you hate me."

"I don't hate you. But I need a place. Like my room, but it doesn't have to be that big. I won't get in it. I just need it."

"A smaller room? Is that what that dome is supposed to be? Some kind of biosphere?"

"Uh huh. But I don't know how to make it right."

"And you can't tell me why?"

"No. Maybe sometime. But now I just need you to trust me. Is it too weird?"

"It's weird. But our life hasn't exactly been textbook so far. Has it?"

"Nope. Ask all my friends who think I'm an alien."

"How do I know you're not?"

"Daddy."

"It would explain a lot."

"I'm serious, Daddy."

"Well, I won't pretend to understand it, but if you want it that badly I'll build it for you. This weekend we can…"

"I need it really fast. It's like life and death and stuff."

Will looked into her eyes, searching for any hint of deception or waver of commitment. He found none and realized his rationalizations were futile. "I'll get right on it, Captain."

"Roger Wilcox, Scotty."

Her smile was payment enough.

The next morning she came out of her room tentatively. She spent so much of her life entering and exiting only after a sanitizing shower or simply being confined to the sterile environment that simply rolling out of bed and walking into the kitchen seemed almost forbidden.

Will was cooking silver dollar pancakes. "Good morning, normal girl. Sit and get ready for my world famous pancakes."

"World famous?" she challenged lethargically as she fell into her place at the table.

"They will be. Here." He slid the first installment onto her plate. "Dig in. Mine are coming and once I start, you're history."

"Ha. Good luck, old man. I'll eat you under the table." Feryl doused the tiny meal with far too much maple syrup.

"Easy there, missy."

"I get to. I'm well now. Unless you're going to put my room back up." She glanced up from her breakfast and stayed her fork to await his response.

Will flipped his pancakes as an excuse to conceal his expression from the child. He spoke without turning. "I meant what I said last night, sweetheart. I'll do anything for you as long as it doesn't hurt you or make you sick again." He turned to look her in the eye. "Letting you go back to that room would hurt you. You need to be out of it. We're done with that."

"You said you trusted me."

"I do."

"Then you have to trust me that I need to have a safe room."

"Even if it makes you sick?"

"I won't go in it. I just have to have it."

"Why have a room you can't go in?"

"That's the part you have to trust me on. At least for now."

"So you want a room that you can't go into?"

"Uh huh. The little one will have to do. You said you'd build it for me." She popped a dripping pancake into her mouth as she awaited his response.

He still didn't understand her counter-offer, but knew by her tone she had no intention of dropping it. "How big?"

"Like an aquarium."

"The biosphere thing. Is that what we're talking about? What do you want in it?"

"I don't know yet. Can I tell you when it's done?"

"Well, think fast."

"How fast?"

"Depends on how hungry you are. I finished that thing last night."

Feryl was elated. "You did? It's built? Where is it?"

"Easy. First breakfast. Then we'll go out to the shop and have a look at it. Then we'll talk. Deal?"

The Seventh Chapter

Feryl examined the heavy dome. It was difficult to see through the textured glass, but Will had taken the initiative of populating the dome with soil, water and a few plants, including a faux bonsai tree, which gave the tiny world a majestic look.

"Is that what you had in mind?"

"No. It's better. She'll… I mean I love it."

"Ready to tell me why I made it?"

"Not yet. I still need you to trust me."

"You're asking a lot. I know something's going on, and I'm a little afraid you're into something dangerous. Give me something here."

"I'm too smart to do something like that."

"You're not that smart."

"Bet I am."

"How much?"

"Tell you what. If I can beat you at pool, will you agree to trust me?"

"How does pool make you smart?"

"You'll see. Is it a dealio?"

Will cocked a suspicious eyebrow at the odd challenge. "When did you learn to play pool?"

"I've been practicing. Deal? Or are ya chicken?"

"Okay, Minnesota Shrimp. One game of rotation. I win and you spill the beans."

"And if I win, you just trust me and do what I ask without being all Spanish Imposition."

He shook her frail hand without bothering to correct her and followed her to the small pool table they had never used. Once in the room he was surprised to see her produce an invention of her own. She had taken the end of a rubber golf club grip and attached two aluminum curtain rod supports to it. She fixed a laser pen light to the base of the brackets and another one at the top. When the gadget was slid onto the end of the pool cue, the bottom laser pointed to the contact point on the cue ball, and the higher one pointed over the cue ball to the target ball. With the shot lined up with a laser sight, she couldn't miss.

She insisted her father break, and she proceeded to practically run the table. It was only her inexperience at the game that gave Will the opportunity to beat her. But he was so impressed with the inventiveness of her gadget, he deliberately lost and agreed to take her on her word no matter what.

"So what did that cost me?"

"You have to just listen and accept anything I say. You don't get to ask why or say you can't. It's really super important, Daddy. Okay?"

Will feared the consequences of the answer he knew he was about to give. With a sigh, he settled into the journey. "All right, sweetie. What's up?"

"Well, you made that little clean room for me. Right?"

"Right. Are you about to tell me why?"

"Not yet. Not everything. I just need you to do more. The world is eating itself. Everything is getting dirty. The air. The water. Everything. You have to fix it."

"You want me to stop all pollution? That's a pretty tall order, hon."

"Not all of it. At least I don't think so. But you have to find a way to stop people from ruining everything. It has to be now. Will you try to do that?"

Will was a bit stunned at the magnitude of the vague demand. "Will I try?"

"To fix it. Just promise you'll try before it's too late."

Will looked into her youthful eyes and saw genuine fear. However absurd or outlandish the request seemed, he knew "No" was not an option for him. He reached out and pulled the child against him to hold her tightly. "I promise, sweetie."

The Eighth Chapter

"Fix it," Will muttered as he sat alone that evening. Feryl had gone to bed complacent he would help her. Now the task was left to him to simply "Fix the world."

That's what she demanded. Not fix a loose switch or broken drawer slide. Fix everything. Fix all that is wrong with the world. He knew he was just one man, far less capable of the task than the combined efforts of all the governments, politicians, environmentalists and concerned individuals in the world. But his word was his bond, and he had to come away with at the very least evidence to show Feryl he had done his absolute best. Anything which looked as though he was merely trying to create evidence would do damage to his image with her that he could not bear. He went forward with zeal no less than that of a man with a prayer of succeeding.

He approached the problem as broadly as was his charge. With a handwritten list of the most common ills of the world, he logged onto his computer and began the arduous research. The list included animal rights, famine, child abuse, war and pollution. Entering the general terms into his search engine, he began to research these ills, methodically eliminating short-term issues and greed-based problems to drive his focus toward those issues which threatened the entire planet or the human race. War was rampant and the first concern as Will had always hated that human attribute, but he resigned himself to place that into the "natural order" category. As long as people disagreed, the lesser intelligent or overly passionate would fight over it, and Will believed his efforts would be better served playing into the hands of human wants. He had to come up with something people would prefer over what they had. Pollution seemed to rise above all else in sheer numbers of topics and concerns. Will categorized them by environment and technology, which seemed to encompass virtually everything he found. From there, he broke the list down into natural causes, population causes and corporate causes.

Charting the damage done over the past several decades, he found that the production of Styrofoam rated high in all the negatives. It was highly detrimental to the environment both in production and in landfills and seemingly easily replaced by less damaging alternatives. Will gave Styrofoam a mental silver star for merit and looked on. He soon began to feel daunted by the sheer multitude of pollutants and the undeniable and preventable damage they did. In most cases the cause was centered around greed and laziness. As with Styrofoam, an environmentally safe alternative was generally available. But industry was not prone to buy an entirely new production plant when the product currently being produced was still marketable. Finding a cost-effective means of converting the existing machines to produce the new product seemed the way to go forward. Will was beginning to get excited about his project.

As he readied his steps, he came across some startling details surrounding the production of palm oil. Clicking the links related to this concern opened a Pandora's Box of issues, seeming to overshadow all else. The more he read about this oil as an alternative fuel, the more he realized how futile any other efforts would be in the long term.

He learned the Indonesian rainforests were being lost at an alarming rate to clear room for palm trees. Big business and foreign governments were bulldozing the precious resource at the rate of four football fields per day with only acceleration on the horizon. Even the extinction of hundreds of known species due to loss of habitat seemed insignificant when compared to the true danger of the environmental projections. The total destruction of the atmosphere could be measured in years, and for the first time in double digits. The human race was killing itself within a single generation. Will deduced from the documented facts and figures that his grandchildren would never reach adulthood.

Why, he pondered, would any rational human lay hand on such a devastating enterprise? As with the previous issues, the answer lay with simple human greed. Palm oil had a number of uses, and all of them could be replaced by another source. Cooking oil and food additives had several alternatives most of which were actually healthier than palm oil.

Will found that the recent increase in the production of palm oil was due to its application as a fuel substitute. People wanted a clean, affordable alternative to fuel, and palm oil was renewable. No matter that it could only replace a fraction of the fossil fuels being used and needed to be mixed with diesel fuel to be practical. The market had presented itself. Profit was there so people would as a whole turn their collective back on the impact. They did not want to destroy the world. They were simply doing what was easiest, and business was selling it to them at all cost.

So the task was clear. He could not stop them with protest or objection. He knew people that well. The ones who tried to stop them had virtually no effect. He had to do what they pretended to do, but do it right. He needed to develop a clean, economical, practical, renewable, and above all, popular alternative to palm oil. Looking at the practical applications for palm oil, he found cooking had been its main application as a food additive or lubricant. The recent surge in demand was due to developments of palm oil as a fuel source. It could be used for heating or for engine fuel by combining it with petroleum additives. While superior alternatives to other applications already existed, the new fuel oil was being touted as the renewable hope for the future. Will found that alcohol or methanol would perform as well as, and in many cases better than, palm oil as a combustible fuel. Alcohol could be made from virtually any organic material, which would also reduce pollution. Why toss garbage out? Put it in your tank. He was surprised to learn that most modern cars were already programmed to burn alcohol, and the older models could be adapted with the installation of a modified microchip or an inexpensive fuel regulator.

While researching the most efficient method of distilling alcohol, Will discovered an article on a recent development. A Chicago research team had engineered a synthetic version of the common E. coli bacteria which could help build a better biofuel. By altering the basic genetic structure of the bacteria, researchers were able to stimulate it to produce long-chain alcohols nearly four times denser in energy than those found in nature.

Will seriously doubted he would be able to quadruple the energy of conventional alcohol in his garage lab, but he could see several advantages to using the longer chain alcohol. In addition to packing more energy per gallon, it would not corrode the engine and would still be compatible with jet fuel or diesel fuel. As this was the first time researchers had been able to synthesize long-chain alcohol, he was only able to hope he could duplicate some of the process in his own lab.

While the exciting development was still highly experimental and existed primarily in the research lab, Will was particularly intrigued by one part of the process. The research team was able to synthesize the alcohol by inserting chromosomes into the E. coli's DNA, which enabled it to overproduce a natural, elongated version of a compound that became an amino acid.

Will could not ignore the correlation between the new alcohol enhancement and his own project. The amino acid was simply an anabolic steroid that pushed the enzyme development. While theirs was organically grown within the compound, he wondered if he could inject an amino acid into some organic material and then distill it to alcohol to produce a similar effect. Steroids were readily available, and the right one could be the accelerator his process needed. So there it was. The designs were common and the necessary elements easily obtainable. Will actually laughed out loud as he created a list of materials and realized he already had most of the components for a distillery in his workshop. A gas cylinder, the burner and electronic igniter from his barbeque, a length of copper tubing, a pressure gauge and a large glass bottle comprised the bulk of his distillery parts. An unsavory morning stroll through the local landfill would give him enough free ingredients to work with.

Will began by injecting a bucket of mashed corn and apples with a strong anabolic steroid he purchased over the

Internet and set them aside to decompose. This gave him time to build the still. The 25-pound capacity Butane tank had to be cut open and drilled for the condensation tubes. He unscrewed the valve on the top and filled the tank with water to eliminate any risk of the tank exploding. As liquid could not be compressed and water was not combustible, he safely cut a six-inch square opening in the top to be used to drop organic substances into the tank. A larger piece was fitted over the opening and hinged to effectively seal the tank. The addition of four coil heaters and a pressure valve completed the tank. It had four exit distillation coils instead of the conventional single coil condenser and could withstand greater heat to accelerate the initial separation.

Once the separation tank was filled with the legally enhanced corn or apples or plain garbage and pure water, the four coils still became an alarmingly efficient, self-propelled fuel factory. It took hours of continual running to triple distill the material, but only twelve percent of the produce was reused to heat the tank. The rest was pure profit, and he had a small, portable still capable of producing two liters of clean alcohol per day on a self-fueled burner.

He drafted plans for an industrial size which could power a fleet of trucks. Planes and boats could use the fuel as well, though jet fuel was still a bit out of reach, at least for the moment. Will built a fuel adapter for older cars and printed an instruction manual on how to distil organics for fuel. After three days of design and construction, it took only two more hard-driven days for Will to apply online for both the design and application patent on the Billings Quad-Coil Home Distillery pack.

Will had no way of knowing that the Library of Congress was continually monitored. Certain claims sent a flag to interested parties. His application and diagram were intercepted within minutes. Will waited patiently for the confirmation to be verified and transmitted to him, totally unaware of the fact that his invention had already been noticed.

In another part of the country, in a well-lit office populated by people calmly sitting at their respective work stations, one computer softly pinged a warning to its operator. The mid-thirties woman broke her conversation with the nearest co-worker and glanced at the warning.

"Got something?" asked the man she had been speaking to.

"Looks like it. Another genius saving the world, no doubt." As she recorded the particular details of the surveillance hit, the man came around to glance over her shoulder.

"What is that? A home distillery? He's applying for a patent on moonshine?"

"Methanol, Billy Bob. The energy flag tipped it off."

"Whatever. So are you going with us after work?"

The woman continued to fill out the digital form associated with the patent application. "Wait. Bear with. Billings. Perpetual... Exponential output... Got it. Let me send this to security and then I'll go."

While test-driving around the neighborhood in his own car filled with his own home-made fuel, Will surmised that he could market the Billings Still for only forty-nine dollars, making it attractive to any level of consumer. For less than the price of a single fill-up of regular gas, one could buy a means of potentially unlimited free fuel for the family car, home heating and cooking. It could even power a generator for electricity. All for a single affordable package to convert garbage. Due to the still's simplicity, Will would see a profit after shipping and packaging costs of fifteen percent per unit.

The QCHD pack in place, Will pondered it for several minutes before daring to admit to himself it could actually work. He pulled his car into the carport and lifted the hood. The car was running a bit lean but still smooth. Nothing was burnt or destroyed.

"Fixed," he dared say out loud.

*****

Channel Four news was buzzing. The financial crisis was leading the way, pushing terrorism and crime to the

61

back burners. Every journalist had a niche and a foothold on a story line. Each broadcast was a new attempt to say what other networks did not know yet. It was a typical news day.

David Mercado poked his head into his program director's office. "You wanted me, Ted?"

Ted pulled a single piece of paper from his desk and held it up for David. "What's this supposed to be?"

David committed to entering and looked more closely at the document. "That's my lead."

"Your lead?"

"Yeah. It's a health care deal. I'm trying to prove that more than seventy percent of the funds going into healthcare are being skimmed. We're talking pools, trips to Bermuda, all the fat cats…"

"We've got healthcare covered. Angie is doing one angle on funding cuts, and Bill is doing one on the elderly."

"But this is different."

"We've got it covered. What about your story?"

"The dog show? I did that one in my sleep."

"Shane said he was sending you to do the British one. Said this was just a warm-up."

"Shane? That putz? Is that how you got this?"

"He's the features editor."

"He's a nosy prick."

"And a putz but he's also technically your boss so you might want to listen to him once in a while."

"I'd rather work. I mean, where did that guy go to school? Did he go to school?"

Ted wiped the frustration from his broad face and gestured to the empty chair next to David. David sat to await the anticipated lecture.

"I know how bad you want to get back into it. You want a big, meaty story. I know you could do it a hell of a lot better than Bill, though if you repeat that I'll deny I ever met you. I remember how you used to be. But you're new here, and everyone above you is under contract. We have to use what we have. It's simple as that. There's a bunch of stories we have to air every day on a range to keep all the viewers tuned in."

"So why the dog show? Anyone can do that."

"Anyone can do the debates. Most of the headline stories write themselves. The lucky stiff that gets to stand there with a microphone and ask stupid questions is only there because she's got a better contract or more seniority than you."

"So you don't just think I'm bad."

"I think all reporters are bad. At least ninety nine percent of them. Even the top ten percent are only imitating greatness. I don't think they know what greatness is. Do you?"

"Do I what?"

"Do you know what greatness is?"

"What? In reporting? Or in news?"

Ted thumbed a remote control and gestured toward the wall-mounted television. David turned to watch a taped news story he almost recognized. The tape showed a crowd of reporters waving microphones at a fence outside a prison in Birmingham. A dark-haired woman was coming out to face the onslaught.

"This is the Blanchard execution," said David.

"Good eye."

"I was there. This looks like just after her son was executed."

"A two-year legal battle to get key evidence presented, and every penny she'll ever see spent for nothing. See if you can count how many times she gets asked how it feels."

As David counted, three out of every four reporters asked that very question. "How does it feel to know your son is dead?" "How did it feel when he actually died?" "How does it feel to know it's finally over?" The question was paraphrased in every way imaginable over the few seconds it took the bereaved Mrs. Blanchard to push her way through the mauling crowd. She ignored them all. Then one microphone emerged from the crowd, and a man asked, "Do you still believe Lionel is innocent?" Mrs. Blanchard stopped and looked up at the man.

Ted pressed the pause button at that moment. "Hear that? That is a journalist. He asked the one question that mattered. Any reporter who can go into that kind of scenario and ask how it feels doesn't deserve a press card. We know how it feels, or at least how it's bound to feel. My God. Her son just got fried right before her eyes. Are there two ways to feel about that? I hate everyone at that release except this one guy. Watch."

He hit the play button again, and the woman looked the reporter in the eye. "You damn right he's innocent. The proof is right in there lying on that desk, and anyone who looks at it knows he's innocent. But that judge decided he didn't want to see it, and that was the end of the evidence. The end of the trial. The end of my son's life." The tears finally came, and the strength left her. She made one last attempt to defend her son by drying her eyes and looking at the young reporter. "How can God let a man sit on that chair with so much hatred in his heart and judge anyone?"

Ted stopped the tape. "That's a story. The judge got booted. The evidence was made public, and you went on to a brief but stellar career with CNN."

"Uh huh. So I've had some ups and downs. I'm thinking I'm due for an upswing pretty soon. So about my dog show."

"I think you could be that guy again. You'll get a shot, and when that shot comes, you need to be on my payroll and in my good graces. If every PM you work for hates you or thinks you think you're too damn good to work your way up, that shot will happen and you'll be covering the flower show somewhere. Get me?"

David looked at the floor. He looked at the healthcare research he had done. He looked at the diplomas on Ted's wall. He had made two decisive career moves he could never take back and had spent the last four years working in hopes the public could remember him and yet forget what he had done.

Finally he looked at Ted. "I think the Great Dane is going to take it this year."

Ted smiled. "Stick it out. Your time is coming. I promise."

David had earned a reputation for attacking cutting-edge stories with an aggressive style. When a local network offered him his own interview show, he debated the merits of abandoning his ideals and future plans for the risk of being compared to Jerry Springer. But he convinced himself he could make it work. He could do what Springer and the rest were supposed to be doing.

David's show gained immediate local attention, and in his second season he was approached for national syndication. It seemed as though the gamble was paying off. Then it came time for the fateful program he had pushed for. He had lined up three pedophiles and their families to discuss the concept of child molesters deserving a normal life.

His first guest, a man convicted eighteen years earlier of child molestation without having served any time, could not appear due to health reasons. But his wife came in his stead to fight his cause. David amended his attack plan.

"Marjorie Carsten. You're presently married to Angelo Carsten. Is that correct?"

"Yes." She spoke in a cautious tone. Mrs. Carsten was a woman in her mid-thirties with a face and demeanor of one many years older. The lines around her eyes showed the weight of the burden carried for half her life.

"And how long have you been married?"

"Seventeen years."

"To Angelo Carsten?"

"Yes."

"The whole time?"

"Yes."

"At what point did you find out he was a child molester?" He continued his interrogation in the smug, confident manner of a slick prosecutor.

"Well I knew about the conviction, but..."

"You knew? Before you married him?"

"Yes I did. You see—"

"What I see and the whole world sees is you condoning possibly the most horrific crime facing our society."

"No. I'm just trying to make the point that Angelo's not the monster everybody's making him out to be."

"Not a monster? A convicted rapist and child molester? You know, I'm a father and when I think of what this ... I'll say it... monster did, it makes my flesh crawl."

"But you don't know what he did."

"He pleaded guilty to child molestation. He confessed. You don't have a problem with that?"

"No. I don't actually."

"Do you think the victim would be so forgiving?"

"Yes. I do."

"You think the child that this pervert molested would have a kind word for him?"

"Yes. It's me."

"What's you?"

"The victim. It's me."

"You? You're the one he attacked?"

"I'm the one he was charged with assaulting. Yes."

"Well, he pleaded guilty. And I understand they dropped the statutory rape charges in a plea bargain."

"Yes. We were told it would be the easiest way to get it behind us. He was never told about what would happen once he was put on the sex offender's registry, and we've been hounded ever since."

David raised his voice passionately. "Oh you're breaking my heart! You know what he did, and he even did it to you, and rather than seek the help you clearly need, you chose to marry this... this man? My God! You're as bad as he is! Maybe you two deserve each other!"

"But you don't understand."

"I don't want to. You both make me sick. This whole thing is sicker than I could have imagined. How in God's name do you sleep at night?"

"Usually in fear. Our windows are broken out at least once a month. I never know who's outside and what they think of us."

"Well, I can tell you what they think, not that you care a lot."

"He's not the monster everyone says he is. That's why he wouldn't come on here today. He knew you'd be like this."

"Oh and you think I'm being mean? I'd laugh if I wasn't so disgusted. How can you sit there and forgive this vile excuse for a human being after what he did to you and then turn around and judge me for being disgusted by the both of you? Do you mind if I ask how old you were when he attacked you?"

"I was seventeen."

"You were... seventeen? During the trial?"

"No. When he committed the crime you and the whole world condemned him for. We were high school sweethearts and planned to get married as soon as we could. My father hated him. He wanted me to go to college. So he waited until Angelo turned eighteen. Then he waited until we were out on a date. He had us followed until we parked, and then the police dragged him out of the car and arrested him. Legally I was a minor for the next six weeks so that was his only window. My father had a lot of influence and saw to it that the judge showed no mercy."

David was stunned. "That was the crime? He never...?"

"That was it. He got a defense attorney who told him he couldn't wait to hear what the inmates did to him once he was locked up. The judge was in my father's pocket, and Angelo was lucky they offered him a deal to stay out of jail. We got married anyway and have never spent a day apart. Because of the pedophile list we can't even have children. He's not allowed to be near them. My father, the courts, the puritan communities... Sorry. The four neighborhoods we've been driven out of, and now you have denied this loving, loyal and very decent man any hope of a real life."

David was dumbstruck. He stood there before her with a microphone in his hand and absolutely nothing to say. After a devastating few seconds of deer-in-the-headlights silence he forced a sound. "I... don't know what to say. Doesn't the register say anything about that?"

"Nothing. It only says he's on it right below the word pedophile. You say you have a child? Tell me how that feels. I won't ever know."

David tried to recover with a bout of sensitivity. He adjusted his tone and knelt near her, but she showed him no clemency. His next guest burned him still further. A convicted sex offender was fired from his job as a civil servant after nineteen years and was campaigning to have his pension reinstated. David tried to present him as an unacceptable drain of taxpayer's money and had surrendered his right to any benefits when he chose to commit his crime. Again his vehement assault backfired. The man had been convicted of mooning a rival school after a football game. He and three friends drove past the other team and mooned them from the car. Nothing more. Unfortunately one of the rival players had an uncle who also happened to be the chief of police in that community and took the act to the hilt. He and his teammates were charged with indecent exposure, which only appeared on the record as a sex-related crime.

At the threshold of greatness, David had allowed the camera and the media to change him into the very thing he hated most. The vile sensationalism that gave legitimate journalism a bad name had never been a part of him, and now it was all anyone knew of him and to make matters worse, he had done it poorly. He tried to console himself with the knowledge that this ugly, disrespectful trait was clearly not in his nature, but the public was less forgiving.

The producer, the assistants responsible for screening the guests, and even the network survived. The public was the angriest with David. His firing the next day was made public, along with an apology to the offended parties. He spent a year trying to regain the public's trust. Ted finally offered him an opportunity to start the slow climb back up as long as he resisted the temptation to be provocative. He was to do nothing on the air or publicly which might serve to remind the viewers of his fateful fall from grace.

David returned to his desk, disgruntled and frustrated.

A co-worker walked past him and slowed. "He buy it?"

"Not even close. He killed it."

"Because of the story or because of you?"

"Doesn't matter. Dead is dead."

The man smiled and patted him on the shoulder. "Shake it off, David. You're good and he knows it. Your break is coming. Maybe not this time, but soon. Trust me." He smiled and left him sulking.

"Big break. I think I need a break." He was considering a

prolonged coffee break when his phone rang. "Features desk. Mercado."

"David. This is Will Billings. Do you remember me?"

"Sure. The inventor guy. What can I do ya for, Will?"

"I've got something new. Something really special. I wanted to give you first look since you helped out so much with that piece you did."

"I'd love to, Will. But we already did it. I don't know if every new invention is going to be news. You know?"

"This one is. I'm not talking about fluff. Do you have a person on your staff that does environment pieces? I've got something they're going to be interested in."

David considered calling Shane. He would likely give the piece to Tracy Underhill, the conservationist editor. Tracy tended to look down on everyone, though everyone knew her greatest asset was her cleavage, not her journalistic prowess. She had a particularly condescending tone every time David spoke to her. She even dared pat him on the head once for making a suggestion during a meeting.

"What have you got?" he asked.

The Ninth Chapter

Karen was a terrible cook. She had very few dinner parties, and those were invariably catered. Her excuse had always been that she had no time to spend around a stove, and it took only two minutes to pick up a phone and order a number four or a number six without anchovies. After three days of trying to work without working, deliberately missing her flight to Barbados and being continually reminded of how empty her non-professional life truly was, she resigned herself to the fact that she would have to eventually do something that had absolutely nothing to do with work. Eating was among those things, though her lack of culinary prowess remained. This was far from the most depressing of her concerns as Karen entered the restaurant across the street from her apartment building.

"Will guests be joining you tonight?" the hostess asked with a broad smile.

"Unlikely. Table for one, please."

"Do you have a reservation?"

Karen looked at her more with surprise than annoyance. It was almost as though she was waiting for the punch line. "Do you have any idea how many meals I've paid for in this establishment over the past year? Most of which without a reservation I might add."

"I'm terribly sorry. But we're really crowded tonight, and we don't have any single tables available at the moment. If you would care to wait..."

Karen took in little after that point as she had glanced over her shoulder to spy two of her office colleagues already seated in the dining room. "Listen. Hostess person. Suppose I join my friends over there and spare you the trouble of trying to professionally do absolutely nothing." The stunned hostess merely nodded as Karen walked past her and approached the table where Judy Barcroft and Campbell Hughes were still studying menus.

"Hey Killer Barcroft. One Laugh. Is this seat taken?"

70

She stood with a polite smile awaiting a response in kind to her personal greeting. Her jovial mood was not reciprocated. The two presumed friends looked at her with dry, emotionless gazes.

Campbell replied in a monotone. "No. Why?"

"Steady there, Campbell. I was just hoping to join you guys." She looked to the woman across from him. "Everything all right, Judy?"

"I guess. Sit down if you like."

Karen tentatively pulled out a chair and slid into it. "You sure I'm not interrupting anything? You guys don't seem quite yourselves." The waitress brought her a menu as her dinner partners silently stared at their own. She elected to limit the conversation to small talk until one of them chose to open up. "So, Camp. When did you get back?"

"From the bathroom or the post office?"

"You were in Asia last month. Am I talking to the right One Laugh Hughes?"

"Oh yeah. Not used to using nicknames, or names for that matter. And hey. Thanks for the half-star hotel in a mosquito-infested rainforest." He had gained the nickname "One Laugh" during the initial stages of their deforestation negotiations. Campbell was constantly joking and playing pranks on his co-workers, but seemed to have only one laugh that came out regardless of the level of humor. The three burst "heh-heh-heh" seemed to cover every conceivable situation. Karen was aware of the absence of the laugh as well as the underlying attitude.

"Sorry. But it was work. I suppose I can't call you Killer anymore either," Karen said to Judy.

Judy closed the menu and looked for her waitress. "Seems sort of silly, really. I didn't kill anybody." Her attitude was as dry as Campbell's. No true hostility or anger. She was simply and purely indifferent.

"Geez. Were you in the same hotel as One Laugh? Or should I say No Laugh?"

"Actually, I was. Vic sent me to close the surveyor's contracts. Real fun place, that jungle."

"Sorry, Judy. I didn't know. But hey, you guys did a

71

great job over there. It paid off huge."

"Well. That's what counts. I'm thinking lamb."

Karen endured the meal and lackluster conversation as best she could. She was home and ready for bed and still pondering the absolute personality drain in two of her most flamboyant friends. Judy was a legal advisor who had earned the nickname "Killer" for her passionate zeal. She less worked on a task than attacked it, usually closing in record time. Tonight it seemed she had finally exhausted her passion. Campbell "One Laugh" Hughes was noted for his sense of humor, but Karen found it difficult to imagine the man across the table from her finding humor in anything. He was not the man who had kept spirits high during the long and arduous hours spent on the project. Something had taken a notable toll on these two. Had she pushed too hard? How many more had been affected? No. It was only work, and they were simply tired. Everyone dealt with the conclusion of a project differently. She was having enough trouble adapting herself. She resolved to let Judy worry about Judy, and she would worry about how to keep busy in the office tomorrow and hopefully postpone the forced vacation yet again.

*****

Will was awakened far too early on a weekday by the sound of pans clattering in the kitchen. He dragged himself downstairs to find Feryl rummaging through the cabinets.

"Why do you hate me?" he said in a gravelly voice.

"I need a muffin pan," she said without pulling her head from the cupboard. "I know we have one, you made me muffins before."

"The chocolate chip ones?"

"Uh huh."

"Yeah. Those were from the store. I lied."

"I smelled them cooking."

"You smelled them microwaving. You were room-bound."

She turned and looked him in the eye. "What about the blueberry ones? I know they weren't store-bought."

Will scratched his head and made a feeble attempt to smooth his tousled hair as he moved toward the coffee pot. "Oh, those. Mrs. Peterman brought those over when she heard you were feeling better."

"And you said you made them? Daddy."

"I didn't actually say that. I just asked you if you wanted some fresh baked muffins."

"That's a lie by emission."

"Omission."

"They made you fart."

"Emission. Anyway. What are you doing now?"

"Making grape muffins."

"You can't make grape muffins."

"Not until I find the muffin tin."

"I mean you can't make muffins with grapes."

"We don't have any blueberries."

"We have bananas. Make banana nut muffins."

"Do I have time?" Feryl asked.

"I think so. Can I help?"

"You can help me find the stupid muffin pan."

Will sidled up next to her to help with the baking. "By the way. I just got to bed about an hour ago. Guess what I've been doing for the last couple of days."

Feryl broke an egg into the mixing bowl and carefully picked out the tiny shell pieces. "Saving the world like you promised?"

"Actually. I think I did."

She turned to look at him with no doubt whatsoever in her expression. "Daddy! How?"

They baked and talked, and Will explained the thought process which led to his creating a marketable home distillery package. After twenty minutes of mixing and cleaning the mess, Feryl slid the muffin pan of blueberry batter into the oven.

"So you did all this without even telling me?"

"The patent is registered, and David Mercado is doing another news piece on me."

"That reporter who went to the store?"

"He said it was just what he was looking for. He said he

wanted something to rattle the cages and that was just the thing. It would help the environment, save people a ton of money and make the oil companies really mad."

"Will they be mad at you?"

"They'll be mad if people buy it. But that's the idea. They have to get mad enough to change. Either way, we win. You win."

"Me? I didn't do it."

"Actually, sweetie, you did. I don't really know what pushed you to this. But you pushed me, and this thing that came out of it is really something special. I'm very proud of you."

Feryl seemed unmoved by the praise and looked into the oven window to see if her muffins were starting to rise. "It wasn't me. Not really."

"So you got the idea from someone else?"

"Uh huh. Someone like me. Someone who gets sick easy. She needed us to do it. Fix the world."

"So is that who you're making the grape muffins for? She a school friend?"

"Not a school friend." Feryl stopped and looked up at Will to gauge his reaction. "She's kind of a magic friend."

Will raised his eyebrows and smiled. "A magic friend? She's magic? Like invisible?"

"Well yeah. Most of the time. At least to most people."

"But you can see her? Is she here now?"

"No. She can't be in here. The air makes her sick. Just like it did me. That's why I needed the room back."

Will was becoming intrigued with her elaborate imagination. "Interesting. Does this friend have a name?"

"Uriel. She's Uriel."

"Like the Angel?"

"I think she is the angel. She's really, really old, but she doesn't look it. She says she's always been here but she's almost done."

"Done what?"

"Living here, I think."

Will listened intently and encouraged her to continue, though still with the attitude that he was hearing a well-conceived story.

74

As long as he was listening, Feryl accepted the skepticism and continued. "The air isn't like it was when the world was made."

"Since when do angels need air?"

"She's not really an angel. That's just what some people call her. They've been called a lot of things: pixies, elves, sprites, leprechauns, sprites. I think they're fairies. That's why they need clean air. We can adjust a little, like when people learn to smoke or eat McDonald's. But the fairies can't. They just go out."

"Go out?"

"Uh huh. That's how fairies die."

"So the fairies are becoming extinct?"

"There won't be any more."

"Well, since we never saw them before, do you think we'll notice?"

"Have you ever seen a blue whale?"

"No."

"What about a tiger in the wild?"

"Been lucky so far."

"So do you believe they exist?"

"Of course."

"But you never see them, and they don't do anything for you. Does that mean they don't have a right to live? Humans aren't the only animals that matter."

"You know most eleven-year-olds don't talk like that."

"Uriel told me lots of stuff. But the most important thing is we need the fairies. It's where we got our magic. The stuff that makes us … you know…us. Without them, we aren't special. We won't know how to love and laugh and appreciate like art and stuff. We don't cry at movies or cheer when the good guy gets there or laugh when a fat kid falls on his butt. Colors aren't pretty. Nobody wants to dance or sing. We're like… alive on the outside but dead inside. Like zombies but not scary. That's what we'd be without them. We'll lose what makes us *us*."

Will went into Feryl's bedroom hours after she had fallen asleep. He had learned to listen for her unusual snore to be sure she was asleep. She snored for the first half-second of every inhale and made no other sounds when she was in a deep sleep. While no sound was not a true indication she was awake, the stifled snore was a guarantee she was sleeping. He crept over to her desk and carefully set the sealed bio-dome where she would see it when she awakened. He had to push her jewelry box aside to make room. Once his hands were free he adjusted the box to ensure it wouldn't fall in the night. The lid was slightly ajar and he glanced inside to assess the tragedy of her sparse jewelry collection. The treasure was only slightly larger than he thought. Amid the few baubles he'd given her and a few hand-made items, he noticed the rough shard of blue glass. Even in the dim light, the glass shimmered with a hue he had never before seen. He reached in and lifted the crystal. The edges were rough as if broken but smoothed with years of wear. He wanted to examine it further but feared waking Feryl so he silently crept out of her room and into his workshop.

On the opposite side of the house and well isolated, he turned on the desk lamp and held the glass up. Everything he viewed through the glass sparkled with prismatic luminescence. He saw an odd green glow move along the wall and lowered the glass to see a tiny moth take wing. He took turns examining everything in the room with and without the shard to note the aura given off.

The night was exceedingly dark. No moon was present, and a blanket of clouds shielded the stars from view. Across the street and one house down, a street light cut the darkness to illuminate its assigned section of the suburban street and a lone man standing deathly still at its edge. The tall man held his long coat closed more for camouflage than warmth as he peered through the window of Will's converted garage. His keen eyes clearly saw Will step near the window and gaze about the room. Even at this distance, the stranger saw the blue crystal Will held in his fingers.

"Bingo," the man muttered, nodding in satisfaction.

He tried desperately to keep a scientific mindset but could not resist playing with the fascinating toy, holding it up to everything he could think of. Between boyish moments he managed to measure the lights displayed by Feryl's looking glass with both the scrutiny of a scientist and the youthful fascination of a child in discovery. The effect was quite remarkable. The natural materials like wood and paper gave off a dull gray-green hue. The inorganic and man-made materials like plastic and aluminum seemed to be in black-and-white showing only shades of gray. But each time he chanced upon an insect, it seemed to glow like a tiny star.

It took Will only seconds to realize that this glass revealed the aura of all things and that living objects were profoundly alight. He looked at his hand to see a pinkish hue blanketing him. He flexed his hand as if he could suddenly feel the aura, though he actually felt only his broad smile. The light in the window began attracting the autumn insects, and a large moth bounced off the glass. The tiny thud attracted Will's attention, and he held the crystal up to the window to watch the light show as the bugs passed.

Across the street, the tall stranger saw him raise the glass and leapt away and down the street as quickly as possible. He knew his own aura would at worst frighten the man, and at the very least alert Will he was being watched. He moved far enough down the street that the neighboring house shielded him from view.

Will's fascination with the glass soon lost out to curiosity. He wondered what type of material could produce such an effect. He lowered the tiny treasure and began looking at it rather than through it. For the size of the shard it was remarkably light, but obviously not plastic. The desk lamp was less than sufficient so he moved to turn on the wall switch which controlled the two four-foot incandescent ceiling lights. He deliberately looked directly at the crystal as he flipped the switch.

From the street, the stranger planned his next move. He would need to approach this man analytically. Present him with a problem and challenge him to solve it. That, he thought, would be his way of getting close enough. Maybe the man would share his discovery with him. That would be the easy way, but far from the only way.

He had only begun to formulate the plan when a thunderous blast lit up the street. The concussion sent him rolling back onto the grass. The tremendous explosion sent debris flying all over the street and a hundred feet into the night air. The brick exterior of the original house survived the explosion, but the wood frame addition that was Will's workshop was completely demolished. No trace of the shop or its owner could be seen through the resulting flames.

The dazed stranger rolled onto his haunches in shock. The house was still burning, and he knew that the seriously compromised structure could collapse at any moment. Standing, he started toward the disaster, but was stayed by the sound of a car racing in the opposite direction. He looked up the street and saw a late model, dark gray car in the next block drive away in noticeable haste.

He was confident he was watching the culprits flee the scene as people rarely ran in groups from a spectacle such as this. Had they time to get into the house first? Had they taken or merely destroyed? Even at this distance and dim light, he made out most of the license plate and knew he could likely catch them if he chose. But at what cost? He surrendered the pretense of choice and raced to the house and threw his shoulder against the front door. His size and momentum were sufficient to unhinge the heavy door, and he tumbled into the living room. As soon as he hit the floor, he heard Feryl scream and followed the sound to her room. The house was rapidly filling with dense smoke, and her cries were all that guided his hands to her.

Feryl, blinded by the smoke, clutched eagerly at the hands reaching from the black cloud to rescue her. She had no other thought than that these were the hands of her father.

The stranger laid her on the grass across the street and stood to look back at what was once his hope. He was left with no hope now that a human might have survived the blast. But the crystal might. He thought for just that instant of the crystal, but the neighbors now coming out and the crescendo of sirens told him his time was up. He left the child there on the grass and walked briskly to vanish into the darkness. He would return to search for the glass. For now, it had little value.

The Tenth Chapter

Karen kept only the desk lamp lit over her desk as if hiding from the rest of the office. In the past, it was not unusual to find her and a barrage of overachievers burning the midnight oil at the office. But this evening eight o'clock found her virtually alone. The mood, not just in her office but seemingly through the company, had changed. The once ambitious and enthusiastic researchers, planners and gainers were merely going through the motions of work in a mechanical, almost zombie-like state. Her project brought a sweep of change to the company, but life should have continued. It did not and no one seemed to care. Still, she attempted to keep a low profile.

She had spent the past few days waiting for a backlash over squandering her plane tickets, but none came. She did not volunteer herself, but surely someone had checked. She was not yet prepared to change companies, but this one was becoming difficult to read. The indifference shown toward her in a working capacity was only slightly more unnerving than their interest in her down time. Work was the key. It had to be. She was feeling lethargic because of the letdown after the merger. They surely felt they had seen the best of her. One cure for all ailments was work. She needed a new project.

She had picked up a *USA Today* on the way in. The headlines were focused on environmental issues, and she scanned the wording in each line for a lead or direction. One story dealt with the development of experimental drugs to reduce the effects of Alzheimer's disease. This ignited a train of thought as Karen knew Global Nortatem subcontracted more than a dozen independent laboratories to develop a broad range of compounds. That might be a hook.

Karen immediately logged on and started listing medical suppliers and research organizations. They all needed a means of producing their product in a more cost-efficient way. She had the means at her corporate disposal. They had already done the hard part. All she had to do was underbid the competition and offer the production under an exclusive contract. How many experimental drugs were ready for mass production? It could actually work. She could do the math on what one hospital could charge for a single pill or treatment and multiply that by billions. Global's cut was attractive, but more importantly, she had a new goal. This would quickly blossom into a corporate cause with her again at the driver's seat. They would surely see her long-term worth in this new project.

"I hope you're booking your car once you get there." The familiar voice was nearly pleasant and assertive enough to pull her eyes away from the screen. She looked up to see Vic Albean settling into one of her comfortable guest chairs. "Because if you're working again, I'm going to take issue with it."

"Well, I am at work. Why would you take issue with one of your employees working?"

"Because this employee is supposed to be on a well-earned and obviously much-needed vacation. What are you doing here, Karen?"

"Relaxing. It's what I do, and I don't need a vacation, Vic. Look at this. Westmeyer is outsourcing three major companies to manufacture their base chemicals. We could pull all of that under one umbrella contract and—"

"Boring. Send us a memo on it when you get back. Now take this," Vic said, tossing an envelope on her desk.

"Tickets, I presume?"

"You betcha. And we'll know if they don't get used, so use them. And by 'we' I mean the guys that tell me what to do."

Karen opened the envelope and glanced at the tickets. "Thursday? And no name."

"Call them and give them your details. Passport number. Name. You know. Confirm who you are. They'll do the rest."

"I was thinking of someplace less... tropical."

"Just go. It's a free vacation."

"I could send the whole board of directors there for a

month on my bonus alone. Quit trying to sell me on the bargain." Karen set the envelope down and leaned toward him. "Vic. I'm concerned. Tell me something that will help me relax."

"Okay... Let's see. Relax, Karen. How's that?"

"You suck at this. In fact you suck at everything lately. What will I be coming back to, Vic? What's next for us? I need to know?"

"I think giving you a project now will defeat the purpose of sending you away. Go away. Then come back. Then ask me that." He stood and turned toward the door. "And quit whatever is it you're doing. We're not interested in anything you do unless you get a tan first." He left her without a goodbye.

Karen stared at the doorway as though something might come through it to change what had happened. She looked down at her fledgling project with diminished hope. They would not even look at it.

But they might if it were already viable and profitable. That was her mistake. She had not set her proposal up properly. She needed to get it rolling. Then bring them in. The tickets distracted her. Could she do this from Barbados? Yes. The research was primarily online and telephone contact. Most of the preliminaries could be done from the lobby of the Hotel Borneos. She began to feel optimistic for the first time in days.

One of the principle buyers was under contract. She needed to know who set the contract parameters, how happy they were with the current deal and if another option could even be considered. If they could be swayed to let her incorporate their suppliers, she would then need to meet with her own manufacturing team. She had to be here. Barbados would have to wait. She then wondered how much time she would have between the flight less her person on board and the corporate intervention. Would she have time to show them a tantalizing deal?

With a goal and a deadline, Karen set to work with renewed fervor. She dropped her new data into a separate spreadsheet which split the contacts into "flagged" export countries and those with a more open agreement with the United States. As the new file opened, she spotted a tiny message in the corner pop up.

"Data transmitted. Receipt confirmed." She was being monitored.

She didn't hesitate to pick up her phone and dial another extension. She waited two rings before a lazy voice picked up.

"I.T."

"Who authorized the Nanny on my PC?"

"Huh?" The tech seemed either drugged or simply half asleep.

"You know who this is?"

"You're about the only person in the whole building working. So yeah."

"So I'm asking you who told you to monitor my PC."

"You know what? I'm sure I'm supposed to be all corporate spy and everything. But really this is kinda crap. Getting yelled at for nothing."

"So what did they tell you to do?"

"Just see if you're working. No biggie. You always are, I told 'em."

"Any chance they said why?"

"Naw. They don't say much around me. Not since I told that girl some semi-secret stuff. I mean, she like goes commando and everything. Sure I'm gonna talk. What would you do?"

"Commando? That matters?"

"Any guy that says it doesn't is a… Let's just call him a liar. But listen. I'm just like you. I just work here. I set this stuff up and watch it. Mr. Albean is the one who said you had to get out before…"

"Before what?"

"Before last week. Is it already Tuesday? Dang. Laters."

"Hey! Don't hang up. Is that the only thing on my computer?"

"Everybody gets monitored."

"Did you come into my office to put it on my computer? Truth."

"I personally didn't. But someone had to set it up. Sounds like they did a pretty bad job if you spotted it that quick."

"Thanks, I.T. Go smoke your lunch."

*****

The hospital had been Feryl's home since the explosion. She was admitted for smoke inhalation, but kept for observation mostly to see how she adapted to the death of her father.

The first day she seemed in shock. From morning until well into the afternoon she did little more than mutter to herself. A social worker and a child psychologist stayed with her waiting for some sign. When she finally spoke, she cried out for Uriel. The social worker thought it might be a pet killed in the fire. Once they had managed to calm her somewhat, Feryl demanded someone search her home for the glass dome in her room. It had to stay near her. In an effort to get her to open up, the psychologist sent a patrolman to retrieve the biosphere from her room.

To Feryl's great relief, the dome was intact. She sat with the dome for about an hour before the doctor returned to check on her. Dr. Brister found her remarkably alert and in almost unnaturally good spirits. She looked up at her and smiled.

"Hello, Dr. Brister."

"Well, you seem to be feeling better, Feryl. Are you ready to talk about what happened?"

"Not really. I mean not with you. No offense."

"So... who would you like to talk to?"

"It's done. I'm good."

Ann Brister gazed at the child in bewilderment. She had a variety of speeches planned depending on how the bereaved child's mood developed. This met none of the criteria. She elected to skip ahead. "So are you about ready to go home?"

The suggestion brought Feryl's mood back down. "Home? I thought it got blown up."

"Well, your old house was damaged, yes. But you've got a new home. And a family who loves you very much. You can go when you're ready."

Feryl was clearly puzzled but asked nothing. Dr. Brister turned and signaled out the door. Pamela came into the room closely followed by Everett.

Pamela pushed past the doctor and ran to Feryl, throwing her arms around her. "Oh, darling. We're here! Don't worry!"

The doctor was prepared for an emotional outpouring, but Feryl seemed to her to react to the visit as she would from an elderly aunt on Christmas.

"Mom?" Feryl asked as though she was not sure. She had only seen her mother on holidays when Pamela was not out of the country or otherwise engaged. Even when her mother was unable to find an excuse to postpone a visit, Feryl tried to get out of it. Despite the obligation of bloodline, they were both generally comfortable with the distance.

"Yes, darling. It's Mother. We've come to take you home... when you're ready."

Feryl looked at the doctor as if demanding an explanation. Dr. Brister had little. "She's about ready, Mrs. Billings-Trudeau. If you give us a few minutes to do the discharge papers, you can take her home with you now."

Pamela turned to the doctor, emotion arrested. "Now? Today? Are you certain? I mean, doesn't she deserve some sort of rehab or something?"

Everett spoke over her. "We're ready when she is. Feryl? Would you like to come home with us, sweetie?"

Feryl looked at Everett, then at the doctor. Then she again looked at Everett and said in a solemn tone. "Please don't call me that."

The ride home was made awkward by Pamela's attempts to whisper to Everett while Feryl sat alone in the back seat. Everett repeatedly shushed her and then asked reassuring questions of Feryl to let her know she was not being ignored. But Pamela seemed to take offense and would go silent for a few minutes before trying again. Feryl heard one of the

84

whispers refer to affording her. After that, Everett silenced the rest.

Feryl stepped into the large bedroom and gazed about. The room was not quite as large as hers, but opulent to the point of pretentiousness. The furnishings looked new, and her things were already there and ready to be unpacked. The room was impersonally decorated. Simple floral prints hung on cream-colored walls. The bedspread matched the prints with a dominant color of burgundy. Feryl hated burgundy. This was not her room. Her room was blue and orange. Her room had her things around it, girl things, child's things. This room could be a hotel room for the look of it. There were no toys or dolls or pictures on the walls that she drew. Every space seemed clinical and designated. Her room had places to put things that had no real place. She felt as though even putting her clothes in this closet would be wrong. The room looked like a display in a decorating store. The only thing out of place was her.

With a sigh, she resolved to adjust and set about unpacking her things. The clothes could wait. She needed to see her knick-knacks on the dresser. The large box labeled "Fragile! This side up!" was first. Feryl carefully lifted the glass biosphere and set it on the end table next to her bed. The tiny plants and moss were still green and growing nicely. The soil was on the bottom and seemingly solid. Everything in the self-contained world was intact, so she continued unpacking.

She took to heart the strength and encouragement she received from Uriel and had yet to shed more than the few initial tears upon learning she would not see her father again in this life. Even when she learned she would be living with her mother, Feryl held back her tears. Her mother had been told by the counselor that she was in denial and would grieve her own way and in her own time, and it was best to let her go with it. Only this day, as she went mechanically through the motions of settling into a new life, of trying to make this new world resemble the one she knew, did the sense of loss start to settle upon her. She felt tears welling and sat on the edge of the bed that would be hers to receive the tears.

"I really wish I could help you more," Uriel said to her. She had been sealed in her protective dome for weeks and was holding her strength better than before. "I thought we were past this."

Feryl looked at the dome. She did not need the shard to know Uriel was there. "I know but still."

"You miss him? Have you ever been away from him?"

"Sometimes I used to stay in the hospital for a long time, and he would come every day but if I was asleep..."

"So he was gone, but still there."

"Is that like now? Is he here now?"

"That which made up his body still exists, but it isn't important."

"Why not? Isn't that my daddy?"

"No. It was simply the body he needed."

"But you said before he was still here."

"The energy that held him together and made him special is still here."

"Really? Where?"

"All around you, Feryl."

"Oh. Like heaven?"

"Think of heaven as outer space but bigger than you could ever imagine."

"That doesn't make much sense."

"You need to keep an open mind."

"I do have an open mind." She sat talked with Uriel for half an hour before composing herself and returning to her unpacking. Her mood was restored, and as was her way, she sang whatever song came into her head to fill the void. And as had always been her way, she preferred her own words.

Everett approached the room fully expecting to hear and respond to sobs of a weeping child. What he heard instead was what initially sounded like *Somewhere Over the Rainbow*. He recognized the tune, but the lyrics were quite unique.

"Soooome day I'll look around and see
a bluebird smaller than a bee behiiind you.
Wheeeeeere Jewish boys say Mossletof
and stupid shows get turned right off.

That's wheeeeere I'll FIIIIIInd youuuu."

Everett came in on that note. "Are those your words, or do you belong to some kind of alternative music club?"

Feryl clearly didn't mind his presence, but she didn't seem to welcome it to any degree. "Nope. Just how I sang it this time."

He sat on the bed next to her. "You know, I'm not planning to replace your father. Even if I wanted to, those are some pretty big shoes. I'll be happy to settle for friend."

"Okay."

"Really okay?"

"Really okay like you just read it from page fourteen of the stepdad's handbook."

"Fair enough. It's going to take some effort from everybody so take your time, honey. I mean Feryl. Please be patient with me. And it may take a bit of fighting, but just be yourself. The mold we had waiting for you isn't going to fit."

Feryl took a moment to assess what he meant. She doubted him, but only because of what she had seen of him. She was on the verge of deciding not to trust Everett when she felt Uriel speaking again.

"He has a good heart. I like him."

She looked toward the dome skeptically, but decided she would give Everett a chance on the strength of Uriel's endorsement. "Does Mom expect me to call you dad or father or Pater or something?"

"To be honest, we haven't talked about that. But I wouldn't think so."

"I'm thinking she would want us to talk like that in public. You know. 'Cause of what people might think."

"You read her pretty quick."

"She's not that deep."

"You need to give her a chance, Feryl."

"Do I? Why?"

"Because she's not going anywhere soon. Besides, she might have a lot of rules, but basically she means well."

"Really? Does she?"

Everett laughed. "I don't know."

Feryl laughed with him, feeling a bit wicked.

"But your dad saw something in her, and he was a pretty smart cookie. That has to count for something. Right?"

"He saw something in everybody. He could make anything special."

"The more I hear about him, the more special he sounds. What was your favorite thing about him?"

"I liked that I could ask him anything, and he'd give me an answer you couldn't get anywhere else."

"Well, we'll leave that crown with him. I'm a doctor-type so I would probably just give you the Webster's definition. Ask me something and see."

"No. That's okay."

"Really. Ask me a question you might ask your dad."

"Okay. Umm. I got one. How come there aren't any monkeys in Ireland?"

"What? Monkeys?"

"Yeah. Like, there's buttloads of trees in Ireland. Why don't they have monkeys?"

"Hmmm. Maybe because they don't have any bananas in Ireland?"

Feryl looked into her lap in clear disappointment.

Everett continued. "No, wait. What if I told you that there used to be monkeys in Ireland? Uh huh. The Irish monkeys, or McMonkeys as they were called, became extinct a long time ago. See, Irishmen are better known for their temper than their intelligence. So whenever an Irish man came across a McMonkey he thought he'd found a leprechaun and demand a crock of gold. The McMonkey, not having any gold, would do what monkeys do and throw a handful of poop at him and the Irishman would then pummel the McMonkey to death. After a lot of encounters, gold demands and poop-throwing, the McMonkeys became extinct, and no one even knew they existed."

Feryl giggled but resisted admitting it was something her father might have said. She thought about whether or not Everett would back her if she broke a rule. In the short time she had known him she had rarely seen him do other than give in to her every demand. The only time she had seen him shown any assertiveness at all was when he was defending her. Feryl recalled him shushing Pamela in the car. It was a small defense, and she wondered where he would fall on a bigger issue. Then she looked at the dome. "Okay. If you can take her, I guess I'll try. Would you help me with something as long as you're here?"

"Sure, Bud. What do you need?"

"Can you move my dome for me? It's kind of heavy, and I don't want to shake it too much. It's for school."

Everett carefully lifted the dome and turned to her. "Where do you want it?"

"On the dresser, over there." Everett almost had it in place when she stopped him. "No wait. It might be safer on the floor. Right there under the window. Wait. The sunlight will make it too warm. Over in the corner. Uh huh. Right there. No. I think it will be better on that other end table. Hold on while I move the lamp. Kay. Set it down. Careful."

Everett patiently carried the dome to every location directed by her with no idea she was deliberately keeping him in contact with the fairy inside. She never knew what effect the contact would bring, but she knew her fairy was incapable of anything but good. Everett deserved a boost. If Feryl was to be in his family, he had to step up somehow. As he set the dome gently into place, he smiled. "Anything else?"

"Nope. Thanks."

He gave her a reassuring wink and left the room, pulling the door nearly closed behind him. Feryl was about to continue unpacking when she heard a familiar tune emanating from the hall. As she bent her ear to listen, Everett was singing "You raise me up.... 'Cause I can't stand a moun-tain. You RAISE me up 'cause I can barely see."

She felt the first sincere smile in weeks cross her face. From the dome, she sensed the fairy ask, "See?"

The Eleventh Chapter

"This is different from any of my other inventions simply because of the magnitude of its potential impact," Will Billings had told David Mercado. "It's different because it's not meant to make the world more fun or more convenient. It's intended to save the world. And it can do exactly that."

David Mercado mentally reran the conversation he had with Will. He remembered the grandiose description of his invention and the claims of monumental impact on the environment. So great were his claims that David was enticed to borrow a camera and meet Will at his home for another interview. This one was not sanctioned by his manager and had no assurance of ever being aired, but both men were willing to attach their hopes to it. Now the reporter wondered if the invention or the death of the inventor was the story.

"So you think this is the big one? The one that makes you rich?" David had asked him from the makeshift studio in Will's garage.

"It's not about that. If it were, I'd just sell it to one of the big shot energy companies and retire."

"So why don't you? Wouldn't they know best how to use it?"

"Because when it flies, it'll put them out of business. No sir. This baby's going to make some big shots very angry. That's why I need it public as quick as possible."

"So I assume you're not giving it away."

"Well, no. But if you could buy a single unit for less than the price of a tank of gas that could fuel your car and maybe even heat your home indefinitely—"

"And you feel this will shut down the palm oil industry?"

"Not on its own. There are too many other uses for the stuff, and none of them are necessary. I plan to commit a percentage of the profits to educating the public on what they're doing when they buy these products. With enough effort and concentration on the people who have nothing to lose by switching away from it, I should be able to minimize the market. Hit them in the wallet. That's the real goal..." David watched the tape of that interview again and again. When he had heard about the explosion, his initial shock quickly gave way to suspicion. The timing was too convenient to be a coincidence. He had not even presented the story to his program director yet. He still could and surely would. But there was an underlying story here, and he needed to know which way to go with it. He began delving into the last days of Will's life, looking for something he could show to anyone who would listen.

He replayed the tape of his earlier interview in Will's shop to look for anything else that could provoke anyone. Will owned the patent on almost everything in the shop and was having trouble giving most of it away. He wondered if Will might have stolen someone's brainstorm, but it was hard to imagine anyone being willing to kill a man and a child over plastic lips.

As David leaned back from the screen to allow his thoughts to flow, he felt a tear in the corner in his eye. There was no denying to himself that this one touched him on a personal level. Will seemed like a good man, doing something truly good. For that he died. For that his daughter was orphaned. The answer was there in those interviews. No. In that one. The one Will assured him would have some major players sweating. Could they have already known what he had done? Could someone in power have sensed a serious threat to his own market? The natural investigator could not bring himself to think otherwise.

The search began with an online listing of corporations which might consider alternative fuels a threat. It seemed odd to him that regardless of how he worded his query, the search engine invariably had either Global Nortatem or Planetary Power at the top of the list. Alternative fuels. Energy comparisons. Corporate energy monopolies. His computer seemed determined to lead him to this one search result.

David further noticed that every article or piece relating to Global began with a reference to palm oil. Palm oil was the big money product Global claimed would revolutionize the energy industry. He read of recent mega-mergers spanning three continents which had pushed Global to the top of his corporation list. He was drawn to a photo of a young woman smiling with apparent satisfaction, though the smile appeared insincere to him. The article gave her a vast majority of the credit for the merger.

As though on cue, Shane chose that moment to wander past his desk. "Anything new?" It was his standard done-to-death opening.

David instinctively switched his screen to an online news site. "Nothing that has anything to do with me. Unless somebody grew a potato that looks like Pamela Anderson."

"Hey. Never joke about her. Besides, it might be a story." He spoke casually but seemed fixated on David's computer. David finally locked the screen. "Coffee time. You buying?"

"Uh... no. I got a... thing." It was as though the spell had been broken. "See you later though." Shane left with an uneasy gait, as though hoping to be asked back.

David let him leave without a thought as to what he might have been looking for. He unlocked his screen and tried to resume his search. Logic and preconceived expectations overrode the seemingly coincidental search results, and David started deleting them to look on. As soon as he cleared the searches, he felt an uncomfortable twinge in his arm. Not painful but noticeably uncomfortable. He withdrew his arm and massaged it, still looking at the picture of Karen Gabriel. The delay gave him time to reconsider, and he decided to focus on her. There was something in her eyes which seemed to beckon him. Dare him. If so many thought she was responsible for so much, she was bound to be a worthwhile starting place. The instant he made the decision, David felt the sensation in his arm vanish. He felt a subtle euphoric sensation course through him and was oddly aware of his own breath, cool and fulfilling as he drew it into his body.

*****

Karen had been keeping unorthodox office hours to avoid drawing attention to her presence. The last thing she wanted was to bump into Vic in the elevator at nine in the morning when she was supposed to be in Barbados. After a week of telling herself she had accidentally missed her flight, she began to wish she had taken it and gotten the distance over with. She would be back soon, and she certainly could have worked on a remote laptop since she had no real project to work on. Research on general topics challenged no security and could be conducted from a hotel lobby, restaurant or poolside lounge. So why, she asked herself, had she been so determined to establish a purpose before leaving? She chose work over relaxing as she always had, but for the first time in her life she regretted the choice.

She had slipped in for a stint during the middle of the day but so feared being seen by anyone that cared that she could not concentrate. Even her business-casual attire felt too enthusiastic, and she thought she would surely be found dodging her mandatory vacation.

Some of her initial research could be done from her home office, but the company security policies kept her locked out of much of their permissions and financial resources. She needed to be in the office, but discreetly. After hours seemed to be a promising compromise.

Karen managed to enter the building at 4:45 relatively unnoticed. Even the few people she encountered on her way to the elevator seemed to care little about where she was going or why. She stood to the side of the elevator door and slipped in only once the people exiting had headed for the lobby. Then she had only to hope the door wouldn't open in front of one of the partners or senior staff. Shielding her face with a folder she pretended to read, Karen held her breath to the thirty-fourth floor.

As had been the case for much of the company, the offices seemed deserted. She breathed easier and walked down the corridor past a few insignificant subordinates and cleaning staff. Turning the corner for the last leg of her journey, she looked down the hall and saw what appeared to be a person hurrying from her office. Karen quickened her step down the hall and found her door locked.

"Excuse me," she said to one of the two janitors she'd passed in the hall. "Was someone just in that office?"

"We haven't been down there yet. Do you need something?"

"No. I just saw someone... never mind." She unlocked the door and went in. A quick glance around told her the room was exactly as she'd left it. Even the trash bin was identical. If someone was in there to do something they were supposed to do, then something would be different. Nothing was. Someone came into her office to do nothing or to do something they did not want her to know about. Driven by suspicion, she moved to her desk and felt the back of her computer terminal. It was still warm. It could have been an innocent use of a computer available because its user was in Barbados. On the other hand, she feared they knew she was here. What were they looking for on her computer? Were they watching her? Did they know she was still in town? Did they care?

Her desk phone suddenly rang, startling her to current thought. After a second of cautious hesitation, she lifted the receiver.

"Hello?"

"Yes." Vic's voice was firm but with no trace of anger.

"Vic? Yes what?"

"Yes we know you didn't go to Barbados. What we don't know is why."

"Because... I have a phobic fear of airline peanuts?"

"We are not amused. Look in your top drawer."

She opened the drawer and found an unmarked envelope. "What's this?"

"Darn it. That was supposed to be obvious. Now I've lost all the drama. It's flight reservations, Gabriel. Call the airline, give them your particulars so they can pre-issue the ticket and be on that flight Thursday morning. And they'll alert us if the tickets aren't used."

"Vic. I understand you're upset, what with you not really

ruling the world and all, but can I at least choose where and how I unwind? I've got a fun little project starting that would be a perfect step down and still make a fortune. Vic? Are you there?"

"Huh? Oh sorry. No. Don't care. Just take the beach thing, and I'll see you when you get back."

She hung up the phone without argument. The planted itinerary explained why someone would have been in her office, but why was the computer on? She switched it on to see if they might have left a trace. The first thing that came up was a short list of E-mails. Five were from recent contacts regarding her new project. Two were from Vic, and one was from a friend in the F.B.I. She started to reply but hesitated, looking at the computer as though it were daring her to try.

She lifted her cell phone and pulled him up in the directory.

"Investigations. Jim Gunn."

"Hey, Jimmy. Karen."

"Hi Karen. Did you get my E-mail?"

"Reading it now. So the promotion is effective next month? Well done. You deserve it."

"I just wanted to thank you again and once again ask you to stop calling me that."

"So are you doing something to celebrate? Party? Buy your wife something?"

"Nothing like that. Just taking a few days off."

"Going somewhere nice?"

"You severely overestimate how much the bureau pays us, Karen. If you could go around the world for a nickel, I couldn't get out of sight."

Karen fingered the envelope Vic had planted. "Listen, Jimmy. Jim. I really do owe you. What if I offered you a paid vacation? Nothing huge. Ten days in Barbados. What do you say?"

"I'd probably say something like... Are you serious? Thank you. Then I'd say that the bureau frowns on us accepting gratuities. So thanks, but."

"So think of it not as a gratuity to Agent Gunn but as a

birthday gift to my old buddy Jimmy. Does that work?"

"Might not convince them. Now if you were to give this to your old friend Tina Gunn, that's my wife, and she wouldn't go without her overworked husband... Now that sounds convincing."

Karen smiled. "Tell Tina I'll E-mail her the itinerary and reservation number after I call the airline and add a plus-one."

She hung up the phone and contemplated her act. Passing a paid vacation was odd enough. Now she was paying someone to take it for her. What kind of Karma was compelling her to stay? She placated herself with the thought that she actually felt more relaxed now. They would find out what she had done, and she would present her pet project and take a short rest in Barbados while they marveled at the prospects of her work. When she returned, she would head the project that would lead to the next. Vacationing during a project seemed to make much more sense to her.

The Twelfth Chapter

The tall stranger had searched longer and farther than he had ever thought necessary and still had nothing. The explosion that claimed Will Billings' life brought another line of hope to an abrupt end. The unnaturally keen instincts of this hunter had never before failed him, but people had become so very diverse and creative that anything was possible, even the possibility that his search was in vain. He could not allow that to be the case. It had to be out there. He needed only one, and all of his instincts told him it existed still. It was hidden from him. Somehow it was hiding or being shielded. If he had any hope of finding it before it was too late, he would need to do something he had never done before. He would have to ask for help.

Mrs. McKibbon was a devoted grammar school teacher who lived for those rare moments when she actually had the attention of a majority of her class. Few subjects held the interest of modern ten-year-olds for long. Action-packed video games, fast-paced commercials and rock videos adhering to the standard rule of changing the screen completely every fifteen seconds or less left little wonder as to why these kids had the attention span of fruit flies. But she persevered in the hopes that one or two were actually listening.

This day was special. With the exception of Kenny Sachleban, who was asleep again, and Augie Cruise, who had been unable to take his adoring eyes away from Jenny Hurt since the second day of school, the entire class seemed to be interested in the lesson, and she lectured with enthusiasm.

"How many of you have ever dreamed of space travel?" Half of the hands went up. "So have I. You know it was only a few decades ago when we learned how to leave earth's atmosphere. Does that mean we were the first generation to think about it?" Many of the kids answered no. "That's right. People have always wondered what it would be like to travel to the stars. Of course, they didn't realize how far away the stars are. Even if we travelled faster than the speed of light, we couldn't make it to the closest star in our lifetime."

"But don't you go back in time if you travel at warp speed?" one of the boys asked.

"This isn't *Star Trek*, so let's avoid those terms. But you're not far wrong. Einstein, way before anyone built a rocket ship, figured out it was possible to go back in time."

"So why can't we do it?"

"Because we can't go that fast yet. See, he explained it like this. Let's say it takes a certain amount of time to travel from point A to point B." She chalked an A and a B on opposite sides of the blackboard and drew a line connecting them. "Now what do you think would happen if you travelled that same distance but moved twice as fast? You'd get there in half the time. Wouldn't you? So if you kept moving faster and faster, you'd keep cutting down the elapsed time. That means the time it takes to travel from A to B. Littler and littler, cutting it in half again and again until you travel so fast that there's no time at all from the time you leave and the time you get there. It's instantaneous. Bang. As soon as you leave, you're there. Like light. Everybody see that?"

Most of the class nodded. Kenny was still asleep and slobbering on his desk, and Feryl sat and stared at her teacher but said nothing. Mrs. McKibbon noticed but kept moving on.

"Albert Einstein put that at the speed of light. Then he wondered what would happen if you went faster still? You're already getting there at the exact instant you leave. So if you went faster you'd actually get there before you left. Imagine that. And the faster you go beyond the speed of light, the sooner you get to the place you haven't even left for yet. Just amazing. Isn't it?"

"So do you get younger?"

"I wouldn't think so. But since we can't go that fast yet, we really don't know." She saw Feryl resting her head on her hand in obvious disconcert. "So who has any questions? Feryl?"

"No thanks. I'm good," she replied unenthusiastically.
"Are you sure? Because you look like you're not quite getting this. Do you want to go through it again?"
"No, thank you. I get it. Really."
Mrs. McKibbon did not want to leave her thoughts in the wrong direction. "Feryl. I know this must be confusing for someone who has been home-schooled, but if you like, we can spend some time on it this afternoon. I just don't want you to miss out on it."
Feryl realized she didn't intend to let it go. "I get it. Really. I understand the theory of relativity, but I just don't happen to agree with it. Okay? At least not for time travel."
Some of the students snickered, but the teacher was less than amused. "You don't agree? We're talking about Albert Einstein here. One of the greatest minds in history. I really think if he says it, we should give it some respect. Don't you?"
"Well, the thing is this. You say it's like cutting time in half. If you go twice as fast, you cut the travel time in half. Right? So you claim you can keep cutting the time in half again and again until there's none left to cut and then cut it again until it starts moving backward. The problem I have with all that is that time isn't a physical thing. It's just a number, like a ruler. That's all. But if you look at it like a physical thing, it still doesn't work. Think of a carrot or something. You cut it in half and it's smaller. So you cut it in half again and again until it's so small there's nothing left to cut. Just like one little atom. Now if you cut it again, it doesn't start growing a backwards carrot that gets bigger every time you cut it. It just doesn't work that way. Physics doesn't work that way."
"Well, let's leave the physics to Einstein. Shall we?"
"I am. See, I read that he hated sleeping. Especially when he was working on a theory or something. He would keep working until he passed out from exhaustion. Then when he woke up the first thing he did was throw away the last notes he made because they were pretty much gibberish, him being all tired and stuff. Well, this is one of those sleep-deprived things he probably laughed at when he was rested,

but he forgot to throw it away. He may have said it. But he didn't mean it. And by the way, there's about a dozen stars less than fifteen light years away, so if we could travel at light speed, we could get there in way less than a lifetime."

Feryl was ready for a rebuttal from her teacher, but was surprised when Josh Carter, a student who had rarely paid attention to her, turned around to face her. "So what happens if you travel at light speed?"

"Probably not much, other than you go real fast. I mean Einstein said that a certain speed was instantaneous, and he called it the speed of light because back then they couldn't measure it. Course we now know that light isn't instant but travels at something like a hundred and eighty six thousand miles an hour. Fast but not instant. So somebody found this note later and went Ooh. Looky what Einstein said. Then they did what you just did, Mrs. McKibbon. You figured if Albert Einstein said it, it has to be right. Right? But it's not. And by the way. Thank you for reminding everybody I was home-schooled. I was worried they might start thinking of me as, like, a normal person or something."

The entire class looked to Mrs. McKibbon for her response and found her indignant but dumbstruck. She wanted to correct Feryl, but realized the class was watching her struggle in vain for a retort that was not to come. Finally she forced a smile.

"I apologize if I offended you. I'm sure we all think of you as one of us. Now everyone take out your math books."

The class obeyed, and neither Feryl nor her teacher took notice of the grin Josh could not suppress.

Feryl could have ridden the bus home, but she truly enjoyed the walk when the weather was nice. Today she enjoyed just leaving school. It had not been a particularly good day, and she hoped the walk would brighten what was left for her. She was still within sight of the school when Josh Carter came up behind her.

"Hey," he said in a friendly but cautious tone.

She turned, but immediately looked down. "Hey. Come to make fun of the bubble freak?"

"I don't think you're a freak. None of us do. Well,

except Jimmy Pierce and Kenny, when he's not comatose."

"Yeah, what's the deal with him? Is he like narcoleptic?"

"What's that?"

"It's a sickness where you can't help falling asleep wherever you are."

"Nah. He's just lazy. But most of us... I mean... it's kinda weird that you had to live in a ..."

"Sterile environment. Glinda the Good Witch of the North lived in a bubble."

Josh continued walking alongside her. "I wasn't going to say that. Is that how you knew about Einstein and that sleeping disease and everything? From reading while you were in the sterile place?"

"I guess. My dad was a big fan of Einstein and DaVinci. I had time and books so it just made sense."

"That's cool, I think. I mean I would probably just sit there blaming my mom and dad or something. You did stuff. Oh sorry."

"About what?"

"Your dad. We all heard what happened. Sorry."

"It's okay. I did what I could in a bubble. The choices were kind of limited."

"Well, I know there's a lot of things you couldn't do. But now you can. And you got to read and learn all that and make yourself all... interesting."

Feryl was unaware she had stopped walking. "You think I'm interesting? Me? Homeschooled bubble girl?"

Josh smiled and looked her in the eye for the first time. "A lot of us do. Except... you know. Kenny thinks you're an alien. But those of us in the human race were wondering if you ever... I mean you couldn't do some things in there but you could still learn how."

"What kind of things?"

"You know. Things that you have to do with somebody else."

"No. I didn't do much of that. Have you?" Feryl asked.

"Have I what?"

"Done much stuff with... other people?"

"Some. I mean not a lot," said Josh.

101

Feryl stood on her toes and kissed Josh on the lips. It was over before the stunned boy had a chance to react.

"There. Now we're even. Do you know how to make brownies?"

"Uh. No."

"Guess I'm one up on you then. See you tomorrow." She smiled and left him standing there as she trotted down the sidewalk.

Once home, Feryl ran upstairs. Uriel immediately noticed the change in her aura.

"Something is different about you, Feryl."

"I had the most awesome day. I corrected the teacher, and everybody heard me. And then Josh Carter walked me home and said I was interesting!"

"And so you are. That's very good, Feryl."

"And then I kissed him! Oh my God!"

"You kissed him? That is a very special day."

"I know. I wish I could tell my dad. He'd be so proud of me."

"I'm sure he would be. I am."

"No offense, but you don't seem like it. Are you okay?"

"Just tired, Feryl. I feel so much energy coming from you right now. Good energy. Clean. I like what this has done for you."

"Me too. Do you think my dad could feel it? Can he hear me? I mean if I say something to him?"

"Feryl. We talked about this. The body your father was in is gone. Only the energy that was in him still exists."

"Can I talk to that?"

"It's not like that. It doesn't stay together. I'm sorry. Your father is all over the world now. The best part of him lives in your memory."

Feryl looked down at the floor. "I really miss him sometimes. I mean you helped me at first. But now..."

"Do something for him. Something he would have enjoyed. Would that help you feel more in touch with him?"

"I know!" Feryl said, regaining her smile. "I'll make Dan Brownies. Daddy liked them. I bet Josh will too."

She stopped at the hall when she heard unfamiliar voices

downstairs. A man was speaking, and Pamela's tone was clearly angry.

"The man is dead. How can you say his life insurance won't cover it?"

Feryl crept cautiously to the top of the stairway and listened.

"All I can tell you at this point is that the circumstances surrounding the explosion have sent up some red flags." Feryl did not recognize this voice, but she resisted the impulse to peek in.

"What circumstances?" Everett's voice was still calm but no less concerned.

"The police are continuing to investigate, but at present it looks like either criminal negligence or suicide." Feryl gasped. The man calmly and firmly chose his words as he continued. "There were several tanks of liquid petroleum gas in the shop. Propane and Butane mostly. That was no place for open flames or cigarettes."

"Will didn't smoke," Pamela asserted as Feryl mouthed the words.

"Maybe he kept it from you, or just took it up. There's a lot of closet smokers out there. They found the burnt remains of a few cigarette butts on the floor and a scorched pack stashed behind the file cabinet survived the fire. He may have hidden it, but he was a smoker. That's what violated the policy."

There was a distinct crack in Pamela's voice. "I see. So where do we go from here? Did he have any assets?"

"Well, the store is hemorrhaging money right now. But he had a sizable trust fund set up for his daughter and control of eighteen patents."

"How much is the trust fund worth?"

"To you? Nothing. It's solely committed to Feryl. Even as her guardian, I'm afraid you can't touch it. The executor is a teacher who used to work with her. One Matilda Brentfield. Will was clear in his instructions that only this person or Feryl could touch the account."

"Perfect. So all we can do is try to sell off those stupid patents. Are any of them...?"

"Sorry. He locked you out of those, too. He actually named you in the will as having willingly surrendered all claim to any of them. The patents belong to Feryl. That doesn't mean she can't sell them. But it has to be her choice. The executor has instructions to release interest or relinquish any of this worth only after Feryl has completed a confidential interview to assure she hasn't been coerced or threatened. If you push her, it ends."

"Brilliant. So I get nothing out of this?"

Feryl could not see the look of genuine disgust in Everett though to her mother it was brutally clear. Pamela composed herself less for her husband's disapproval than concern that this agent might still hold some sympathy for her, and she did not want to alienate him just yet. She addressed the agent anew. "I'm sorry. That must have sounded terribly insensitive, but I'm truly concerned for Feryl."

"Feryl?" he echoed. "She's fine."

"She has a chronic illness that's only in recession at the moment. A child is a costly undertaking even if you're ready for it. We weren't, and the majority of our assets are committed elsewhere. Isn't there any way to release some of these restrictions for her sake?"

"Only she can do that, and I have to warn you again against putting any pressure on her."

"I'm allowed to ask her. Am I not?"

"Think of it as a password. You ask wrong, or she feels pressured in any way, and it can lock everybody out for the next eight years."

Feryl slipped back into her room as silently as she could. Uriel could sense little beyond the walls of the bedroom as her receptors were limited by her weakened state and the solid construction of the bio-dome that had become her world. She watched Feryl come back in and instantly saw something new in her aura.

"What happened, Feryl?"

"I'm not sure. My mom is arguing with a stranger about my dad and his stuff. I think it's about me, but not something I did. Does that make sense?"

Uriel used Feryl as an antennae to feel what was going on and why it altered her aura so. "You need to be very careful, Feryl."

"What? What's happening?"

"I can't tell. What I can see is trimutes in your aura. That's never good."

"What are trimutes? Is it something from me being sick?"

"You don't have a human word for it. Think of it as something you have that you don't really want, but someone else is pulling away from you. Like greed, jealousy and coveting all mixed together. If they take it, you'll be hurt. You can't let them."

"Them?"

"Her, I think."

"She? My mom wants my triangles?"

"Trimutes. I see them as tiny jewels floating around you. They don't do anything, but if you lose them, your aura will be very weak."

"Like a hole in the ozone layer?"

"Just like that. And just as important."

"So I need to protect these things even though the person wanting to take them doesn't know what they are. Can I just stay away from her?"

"There's more. Remember a few minutes ago when you decided to do something for your father? Do you remember how you felt?"

"Uh huh. I think it felt good."

"It did more than lift your mood. It changed your strength. This tells me that something very big is happening, and you have the power to stop it."

Feryl was becoming frightened. Uriel had never wasted words or alarmed her needlessly. "What's going to happen? What do I need to do?"

Uriel sat on the soft soil of her tiny world. Reaching out and the emotion that it wrought had weakened her greatly. "I wish I had the strength to help you. I don't. I can only tell you that whatever is in the air around us all was pushed back when you thought of something positive. You need to do something bigger than brownies. Bigger than you. More than you will be saved."

"I don't know if I understand, but I'll try. Right now I want you to sleep. Okay? You look real tired so rest. I'll tell you what happened when you wake up."

Uriel lay down on the grass. "Thank you, Feryl. I love you."

The agent left with the papers signed, instructions delivered and Pamela seething. Everett knew she would not easily let it go and watched her as closely as possible. But he had been neglecting his duties to his practice, and he was forced away for the rest of the day. During the remainder of the afternoon, he divided his attention between his patients and his private studies. His receptionist knew he was distracted, but did her best not to speculate when he asked her to get his accountant to drop by his office that afternoon.

At home, Pamela spent the day bonding as best she could with Feryl. She tried to work money or hardships into every conversation, hoping to lead the presumably innocent child into offering aid. She grimaced while taking out the components of her dinner, clearly sad that there was so little left. She examined her shoes as though they were badly worn, but would have to last a bit longer. She urged Feryl to brush her teeth and take good care of them because dentists cost a lot of money.

Feryl took each subliminal message in stride and responded only to the surface meaning, assuring her mother she would take care of her teeth, and food was not an issue, as she had learned a lot of cost-saving tips she could share. She was more concerned with Uriel's challenge and what big thing she could do and elected to reserve comment on the practically new designer shoes her mother felt had so little life left in them. She deliberately left Pamela with nothing to hope for.

It was late in the afternoon when Feryl heard a soft knock on her bedroom door. Pamela pushed her head in. "Honey? Can we talk?"

"Uh huh," she said, averting her eyes away from her bio dome.

Pamela came into the room and cautiously approached the child. She sat next to her on the bed with such reluctance that Feryl could not pretend not to notice.

"What's wrong, Mommy?"

"Honey. You know we love you and want you here. Don't you?"

"I guess so."

"We do. But I think you're grown up enough to know that things cost money. Some things cost a lot of money."

"Like your car?"

"Yes. That would be one thing."

"Good thing you already have one. Huh?"

"Well... yes. But I was—"

"And Everett's makes two."

"I know but there are other things. Like medicine and clothes."

"And jewelry?"

Pamela tried to hide the rings adorning both of her hands, but could do little about the pearls around her neck. "Right now I'm talking about necessities. The things we're going to need over the next few years."

"I'll help, Mommy."

"You will?" Pamela felt a ray of hope well within her. "You'll help us?"

"Sure. I'll try not to get sick again, and I don't need any toys or stuff. Not even for Christmas. Will that help us out?"

Pamela could not be certain if she was being toyed with, or if the child was truly naive. She knew only she had opened the door and one wrong word could close it. If it closed, she could be locked out until Feryl turned eighteen.

"That... would help. But I'd rather you not have to do without such things."

"Oh I don't mind." Feryl picked up a length of purple ribbon and playfully twirled it around her finger.

Pamela spent another second choosing her next line. "I know, dear. And we love you for your courage and sacrifice. But you've been through so much already. I simply can't allow you go through life without the things a little girl needs. I've made a commitment to you, and you'll have all the advantages the other girls have... no matter what."

Feryl looked up at her in mild confusion. "No matter what?"

"Well, if we have to do without some things or let some of the bills fall behind, I suppose that's the price you pay for parenthood."

Feryl glanced down at her dome for a second. As if being fed intelligence on a subject hooked to a polygraph machine, Feryl was able to know true motives and any untruth told in an instant. She looked up at her mother. "Really, Mommy. I don't want you to do that."

"Really? Do you mean that, darling?"

"Sure. I'm totally serious."

"Well, you know there is an option. But it's completely up to you."

"What?"

"I'm sure you know your father had a lot of things that aren't worth much to you or any of us. But some of them can be sold to someone who might be able to use them."

"You want to sell Daddy's inventions?"

"Some of them. If we can find someone who's interested of course. And the store is costing a fortune. If you allowed that to be sold it would give you money instead of taking it away. Think of it as one less thing to worry about."

"I wasn't worried. But I guess it wouldn't be the end of the world. I mean the store would still be there. Just not ours."

"Now that's my little trooper talking. I'll call Matilda and we'll get started. Is there anything you need, darling?"

Feryl thought. "Can I get a real bonsai tree?"

Pamela smiled broadly and gave her daughter the firmest embrace Feryl could remember receiving from her. "Let's just see, shall we?" She rose and left Feryl to play with her ribbon while she hurried downstairs to begin making arrangements.

She had padded along the thickly carpeted hall and down the stairs before Everett quietly emerged from his bedroom. He had overheard the entire conversation and went into Feryl's room.

The Thirteenth Chapter

Mike DeLago was led into the large foyer of the opulent manor by an appropriately dressed maid. The statuesque woman standing across the room with her back to him did not immediately react as the maid announced Mike and then left him there. Mrs. Jacqueline Van Der Hausen finally turned and slowly donned the forced and unconvincing smile of greeting.

"Mr. DeLago. How good of you to check in. More research? Or have you finally accomplished what you were hired to do?" Well into her fifties, the cosmetic efforts to stave off the ravages of time were evident in the tightly drawn eyebrows and corners of her mouth. The surgical procedures and professional paint job did little to mask the plastic-like skin. For all her efforts, she looked less like a well preserved woman of fifty-seven than a poorly presented woman of seventy failing her attempt to appear thirty. The sleek figure helped, though not so much as she thought.

Mike clearly took no offense at the jibe. "I think I've got something you might be interested in. Would you mind if we went upstairs?"

Her smile quickly faded. "Of course not. Why would I mind?" She gestured up the stairway with an exaggerated wave of her heavily bejeweled hand, and they walked up to the master bedroom.

As they entered the luxurious suite, Mrs. Van Der Hausen made a subtle but elegant gesture toward her husband's wardrobe. Mike ignored the direction and casually strolled toward the bathroom.

"I got all I could from his clothes, which wasn't much."

"Then why are we here?"

"You remember what I said when you hired me?"

"Vaguely. You said so many things. You hadn't investigated yet, so it had little relevance."

"I said that any time a woman thinks her husband is fooling around, ninety-nine percent of the time she's right.

It's just too hard to hide." He continued into the bathroom as he spoke. "I went into this with a totally open mind, but not much doubt. I followed him everywhere. Listened to his calls. Checked his Internet activity. I mean, this guy was really playing it cool. The only woman he went anywhere near was his secretary."

Jacqueline gazed at him and let her eyebrows rise as far as clinically possible.

Mike sat on the pearl-covered toilet seat. "Relax. She should've retired three years ago. Your husband kept her out of loyalty. In fact, didn't you even hire him a sexy young replacement?"

"She was an anniversary present. Very highly recommended. But he let her go."

"Uh huh. Well, that was about the time I came over here to check his clothes. A movie ticket, a perfume, a phantom stain that shows up under a black light. Clean as a whistle. I felt like I was investigating Gandhi. But I had a gut feeling something was wrong. I just knew it. Did you ever feel like that? Like something was... not right?"

"Are we going somewhere with this, Mr. DeLago?"

He looked up at her with the closest thing to a smile he could muster and pointed over his left shoulder to the porcelain handle. "While I was up here, I had to take a coffee break, if you know what I mean. When I flushed, I noticed these. Here. Look at these marks."

She came closer and followed his finger to several tiny scratches on the handle. "I'm afraid I'm not following you."

"I've seen marks like these before. They're made by a man's ring."

"Fascinating. You can tell that from a scratch? Can you guess his weight as well?"

"See, when a woman flushes, she uses her fingertips. But a man tends to lay his hand on the handle. Only a man would put enough of his hand on this little handle to scratch it with his ring."

As clever as he thought that bit of reasoning was, his client was clearly unimpressed. He came forth with the rest. "Okay. So you're thinking your husband probably used this more than you did. But your husband didn't make these scratches. He only wears two rings. His wedding ring and his Phi Beta Kappa ring. Both of them are gold, and gold is too soft to scratch this surface."

He saw her begin to finger her own rings. "Nope. Yours are gold, too. No, this fellow was wearing a titanium ring. The color and fineness of the scratches proves that. So I wondered who wore titanium on his right hand. I looked everywhere. I even looked up that secretary he was so anxious to get rid of. The one you hired for him? I followed her right back to her agency. Nice place. Two-drink minimum and ten-dollar lap dances."

His client somehow managed to maintain her stately poise. "As she never actually worked for him, I can't see how that matters. But I was…"

"It was just a little piece of the puzzle. It told me you wanted him to cheat. That usually means you want to catch him at it. You wanted it bad enough to dangle that thirty-six double-D bait in front of him to set him up. Why, I thought? Well, that one is usually obvious, but I looked anyway and sure 'nough. Turns out you signed a pre-nup. If you leave him, you leave everything. But if he's unfaithful… so what was the rush, I thought? He seems like a nice guy. Hard working. Loyal. Works out and cleans up after himself. I really might have missed it if not for these little gray scratches. See, his partner, Kyle, wears a titanium ring. And Kyle almost never works late. He's so rarely at the office in the evenings that he had the security service text him every time the alarm was set at night. Interesting. Don't you think?" By now, she was rigidly stern, but said nothing.

"So every time your loyal hubby was working away, Kyle was here safely flushing this very toilet. And he got a text from security to tell him when to button up and fly. Beautiful setup."

"I haven't retained you to be vulgar. Nor have you been hired to investigate me," she said, her anger held behind a tightly clenched jaw. "I agreed to the relatively handsome salary you demanded, as I was told you were unusually skilled and of the highest integrity. But for what you ask, I see nothing in return and frankly, I'm extremely disappointed. You're dismissed, Mr. DeLago. And consider yourself paid in full."

"Oh, I don't think so, Mrs. Van Der Hausen. My retainer didn't go very far. The bill is a straight fee plus fifteen hundred a day for expenses. So I'm looking at an outstanding balance of twenty-two grand."

"Are you attempting to blackmail me, sir?"

"What? Like pay up or I'll blow the whistle? Lady, I couldn't care less about your sad little affair. If your husband's partner wants to go antiquing, I figure he's doing Mister a favor. Burning the other end of his candle. Truthfully, the only thing that matters to me is paying my bills and replacing the chair my dog is eating even as we speak. So if you can't find your checkbook, maybe your husband can. Or should I ask Mr. ummm...?" He flushed the toilet as a reminder.

Mrs. Van Der Hausen finally released an actual smile. "I'll be Goddamned. Two hundred and sixty-five million dollars lost over a five-dollar handle."

*****

In the few weeks since having a blossoming adolescent thrust upon him, Everett had adapted to parenting with a natural ease. While Pamela stressed over the details, doing a poor job of suppressing her sense of invasion, Everett seemed to rise so uncommonly well to the task that it was as if he was ready for parenthood all along.

His comfortable, welcoming attitude helped Feryl adapt to the drastic change in her environment. She almost looked for time to sit and miss her father but Everett remained vigilant and positive in his endeavor to keep her moving forward. He included her in everything possible, from housework and home repairs to his daily work and patient issues to which tie to wear, and seemed to value her opinion nearly as much as did Will. She seemed comforted by his attention but more importantly it served the intended albeit obvious intention of keeping her mind off more depressing issues. Keeping her spirits up was his main priority, but whenever all three of them were together the goal seemed to shift as Everett fell into survival mode.

Feryl had a doctor's appointment, and he was preparing to take her. Feryl was ready and at the door as Everett came out of the den with her medical records.

"Ready?" he asked her in a playful, mock-pilot voice.

"Roger Wilcox," she said and opened the door.

"Are you leaving now?" Pamela called from the kitchen.

Everett cringed and looked at Feryl with a grimace. "Yes! We're late so I'll talk to you when—"

Pamela came out to stay him. "I need you to stop at Lucek's Butcher shop."

"Can we do it when I get back? We really have to go." He was inching out the door Feryl held ajar but Pamela did not seem to take notice.

"They close at five today and I need the chops for dinner. I think that's about all."

"Fine. I'll go on the way back—" He tried again to back away without simply cutting her off.

"Now get enough for seven. We've got Harold and Fran and now the Westons are coming. If he has..."

"Seriously Pam. We're late. I have to go right now. Just text the list to me."

"... the seasoned chops like we got last time you should get those. I'd better check to see if we have the vegetables."

"Right now. Us going. Can you hear me?"

Pamela was walking back into the kitchen with a scarcely discernible sense of urgency. "As long as you're going to the store you might as well get the rest of the things." She noticed the wine rack was depleted. They were not normally wine drinkers, but she liked the looks of an extensive selection. Everett was something of a bargain hunter, a terrible trait when it came to selecting wine, and this was not an area she could trust him in, so she elected to make a list. They kept a notepad near the back door to write down anything needed on the next shopping trip and the top sheet was already partially filled. She added three specific bottles of red and three white and then glanced up at the spice rack to check for anything else she might have overlooked. It was then her attention was drawn to the window. From the kitchen she had a view of the driveway where she saw Everett opening the car door for Feryl.

Feryl found her seatbelt and buckled in while Everett rounded the car. He was nearly within reach of the door handle when Pamela came out.

"Excuse me. I was talking. Do you just walk away when someone is speaking to you?"

He looked back at Pamela. "I told you we had to leave. We're supposed to be there five minutes ago."

"So nothing I say matters?"

"I have to go. That's all. Can you understand that I have less than no time to—"

"Do you realize how annoying that is? To have someone just ignore you or cut you off in the middle of a conversation?"

Everett was beaten. "Get in. You can explain on the way."

After another few minutes wasted while Pamela amended her make-up, found her purse and decided whether or not the top she had on was presentable, they were finally and at long last on the road. Pamela was again annoyed that Everett refused to stop at any of the suggested sites along the way to allow her to "pop in for a sec" but endured the ride to Feryl's doctor.

The routine visit was more of a check on Feryl's mental stability than her physical state. Her childhood illness showed no signs of resurfacing, but the doctors who knew her feared she was repressing her feelings about losing her father. Considering the closeness they shared, she seemed far too well-adapted, and this suspected denial was certain to manifest into something more chronic later if it was not brought to the surface now. After another interview, the doctor again concluded she was, for the moment, fine, and merely scheduled her for the next visit. Then it was on to shopping.

Grocery shopping seemed a safe and sedate outing for the family and Feryl thought back to the many times she wanted to accompany her father. It seemed like such fun to wander through the vast selections and try to choose one cake or breakfast cereal over another. Her father was gone, but the store was still there, so joining Everett was sure to be at the very least interesting. Her mother in tow made the excursion slightly less inviting, but she resolved to make the best of the adventure.

She buckled herself into the back seat as her new parents settled into the front. Everett started the car and prepared to back out of the parking spot. All seemed well until the car began to move. At that instant Pamela looked at him and shouted, "Everett!"

He immediately stopped and looked at her to find out what was the matter. She merely stared at him wide-eyed. He glanced around the car to see if he was backing over a child or off of a newly-formed cliff but found no immediate reason for concern. "What?" he asked.

She rolled her eyes and then glared at him angrily. "Everett!" she said again, as though he should have already realized the atrocity of his blatant error, but she again offered no further explanation.

"What?" he again demanded. "What am I supposed to be doing, or not doing? Just tell me."

She seemed so totally disgusted that she could not bring herself to respond to this absurd question and simply adjusted herself in the seat. "Nothing. Just drive, and try to be careful."

Still on edge from the unresolved warning, Everett decided to accept the silence as a victory of sorts and began again to back out. He tried not to react to her poorly-concealed fearful gasp and continued back and out into traffic.

The grocery store was everything Feryl loved about a store. It was vast and wrought with variety and selection. Colors, sounds and smells filled her senses as her imagination had once tried in vain. She found every type of food imaginable broken down into categories ranging from generic labels to gourmet. Everett took the time to read the labels on many of the items. He often asked Feryl's opinion but alternated concerned questions about her diet and special needs with jokes such as whether or not she was allergic to monosorbicglyristerides. She giggled at the obvious puns and took the protective questions in stride.

Pamela, on the other hand, was in no mood for fun. She talked almost continuously and even asked Everett his opinion, but never truly listened for a response, and for the most part answered her own questions. In the dairy aisle she passed the whole and 2% milk and checked the expiration date on a plastic bottle of skim milk.

"Do you think this is a big enough size?"

"For what?"

"For you. You're the one drinking it."

Everett rubbed his forehead in frustration. "I told you last time, I don't drink it. I'm intolerant."

"Well, that's why you make us buy the skim milk. I'd prefer whole milk but you can't drink it."

"I don't drink any of it. Buy what you want."

"And then listen to you whine about how there's no milk? No thank you." She set the skim milk in the shopping cart. "And this time you better drink it. I'm tired of you making me buy it just for you and then watching it go off because you don't even touch it."

"Pam. I'm not going to touch it. I keep telling you that and you keep buying it. Don't buy it for me. Don't buy it at all. Please."

"Oh, you're being ridiculous. Feryl? Do you like chocolate milk? Of course you do." She sat a smaller bottle of chocolate milk next to the skim milk and shopped on. They had a similar discussion about tuna that carried Pamela to and through the checkout stand.

The entire time they stood in line, Feryl watched as her mother continued to browbeat Everett over the tuna and the car and his clothes and the butcher that was now closed and everything she could dig up. She seemed to have an endless arsenal of wrongs to hit him with. Feryl wondered how he so calmly endured the verbal thrashing. She looked up to see him in an apparent trance. His eyes stared straight ahead without so much as a blink. He was clearly miles away, she thought. He might be thinking of a desert island where he was king of the castaways. Or possibly a football game, with him calling the plays to win the game. He might even have been playing his favorite movie in his head. He was obviously not here.

They moved close enough to begin unloading the selections onto the conveyor. Pamela reached in to pick up the first item and Feryl wondered if he could hear them at all. She had her answer as he slyly shot her a glance and a quick wink. She smiled. He knew, and now she knew.

As her parents unloaded the cart, Feryl glanced at the stories gracing the front pages of the tabloids. The Loch Ness Monster had apparently been found again. Cancer had been cured by eating live goldfish and scientists were baffled. Bigfoot had fathered another child and Britney Spears was provably an alien. Some of the lesser stories had some foundation in fact, but were less likely to sell papers, so they were downplayed and only printed in order to claim some measure of credibility. One such article brought Feryl to lift the paper and read.

A young boy used the insurance money he received from the "accidental" death of his parents to track down their killers. The "Baby Bounty Hunter" as he had been dubbed had hired a private investigator to prove that the accident that cause of his parents' deaths was not due to his father's negligence but someone else's. The mechanic who last fixed the brakes had neglected to tighten the fittings and the lost brake fluid proved to be the true cause of their death. The boy used what was left of his money to hire an attorney and sue the national auto repair chain for a huge settlement.

As she read, Feryl felt she had hit on exactly what she needed. This fit perfectly with the challenge Uriel had given her. She had it.

They were home and the groceries unpacked before Pamela realized Feryl was missing. "Where did she go?"

Everett had seen her dart up to her room the instant they got home but said nothing. He could hardly blame her for doing exactly what he wished he could do. "She's all right. I'll get this."

"She needs to learn to pull her weight around here."

"She's a child. She doesn't weigh much."

Pamela lowered her tone. "Well, she costs much. We need to find a way to free up some of Will's assets. We've got bills to pay."

"We're fine. We always have been. Just drop it."

"I beg your pardon. I will not just—"

Everett turned to her and closed the distance between them with an air of assertiveness unseen before. "Yes... you will. Leave her alone."

Pamela was dumbstruck by the turn but gave no ground despite offering no rebuttal.

"Unless you're planning on acting like her mother, just get off her back." He stared at her long enough to send the message and gain confidence the message had been received.

Feryl was on a mission. In seconds she had logged onto the Internet. Whether or not the story of the baby bounty hunter was true, the inspiration was very real. In her search engine she typed "Private investigator." The selections were endless but the journey had begun. She opened the first listing and read.

She scanned for catchy phrases such as "The hardest are the best," or "Specializing in unsolved crimes." One agency seemed to pop up most aggressively but said very little. She deleted the ad for "Blue Lake Investigations" and filled out the on-line form for "Third Eye" simply because the name sounded like fun.

Pamela kept her hostess face on during their dinner party and excused Feryl to have her dinner in her room. She stayed upstairs and out of the way during their dinner party. Everett checked in on her from time to time but believed she was happier spending time with her thoughts.

The next day they all spent time on their own. Everett was called away to the hospital for a few hours while Feryl continued to search online. Uriel seemed disinterested in her project and spent most of the day resting under her tiny tree. Pamela interrupted her only twice, once for lunch and later for supper and otherwise busied herself downstairs all day.

Pamela found it difficult to enjoy her dinner that

evening. She was distracted by her watch and the sound of any passing car. Everett and Feryl offset her preoccupation with their calm, almost jovial, demeanors.

When the doorbell finally rang, Pamela grinned and put on a surprised expression. "Oh. Who could that be?"

"Maybe one of us should go find out," Everett suggested.

He had never seen her so unhesitant as Pamela stood and headed for the door. He and Feryl exchanged knowing glances but said nothing. It was only a few moments before Pamela led Matilda Brentfield into the dining room.

"Feryl, honey. You remember Matilda, don't you?"

"Uh huh. Hi Matty."

"Hello, Feryl. You're looking so grown-up."

Everett stood. "Hello Matilda. Can I get you something?"

"Just coffee please. I've had my supper."

Everett stepped to the sideboard and poured a cup for their guest. "To what do we owe the pleasure?"

"Well, I'm told Feryl has made some decisions about her father's assets. Is that true, Feryl?"

"Yup. I know exactly what I want to do."

Matilda sat down near her. "You do?"

"Yup. It's about Daddy's patents and store and stuff. We need to sell some of them."

Everett glanced across the room at Pamela. She stood silent but her body language told another story. She was pursing her lips and repressing a smile of anticipation. Her hands opened and closed as though she could not decide to make a fist or wave. Her eyes were fixed on the conversation and jumped frantically from Feryl to Matilda and back.

Matilda looked up at them. "Would you mind if I spent a few moments alone with Feryl?"

"Of course not. You can use the study," Pamela said in an overly pleasant tone. Following her gesture, Feryl led Matilda out of the dining room. She glanced back once to see her mother's reassuring nod. With another brief glance at Everett, who merely smiled confidently, she took Matilda into the study and closed the door.

"So," Everett said. "This is kind of out of the blue. Is it something she came up with all by herself?"

"Of course," Pamela responded, feigning indignation. "You know as well as I we're not permitted to influence her. The child simply knows right from wrong. That's all."

"Is it?"

The secretive meeting lasted much longer than either of them had anticipated. Everett stayed his nervous wife from intervening by assuring her they were probably just catching up. Matilda was a friend of Will's, and they surely had a great deal to discuss. Still she paced anxiously for most of the twenty-five minutes Feryl was away.

Finally the door opened and they emerged hand in hand. Matilda was carrying a stack of hand written notes.

"Well, I've got a lot to see to."

"How did it go?" Pamela asked.

Matilda looked at her young client who merely nodded in approval before responding. "Feryl has been doing a lot of homework on this, and she's taken what sounds like very good advice. She's asked me to look into selling the store and several of her father's patents."

"That's wonderful!" Pamela exclaimed, unable to contain her elation.

"That's right. She's thinking about the future. Impressively, I might add. She's arranged for all of the proceeds to be invested in securities and fixed-interest Treasury bonds. By the time she's ready for college she should be a very wealthy girl."

Pamela's mood instantly changed. "What? But what about now? Will she have access to any of it now?"

"She doesn't need it now," Everett interjected.

Pamela looked at him and realized what had happened. Feryl had done exactly as she was advised. But the advice she took was from Everett, by way of his investment counselor.

Feryl was extremely pleased with the outcome. "Banks and the stock market are shaky right now," she said as though reading a script. "We're going for an FDIC-backed portfoliator."

Matilda snickered at the comical effort. "I should tell you both that in my opinion, she was very clear and lucid in her intent and reasons. She even taught me a few words. I'll run it by my broker first to confirm the actions are sound, and to see if he knows what a trimute is, but please don't ask her to change her mind."

"Wouldn't dream of it," Everett assured her. "Would we, Pam?"

Pamela was livid, seething with rage and doing a disastrously poor job of concealing it. "Whatever she wants," was the only reply she could muster before storming out of the room.

Everett tried to hold his polite smile but flinched a bit with the thunder of a slamming door. "I'm going to pay for that one later."

"You did the right thing," Matilda said. "Now her money's assured and safe. Thank you."

"Yeah, thanks," Feryl echoed.

The Fourteenth Chapter

Mike DeLago came home to work, as the office was distractingly sterile when he was between jobs. He normally avoided allowing work and home to mix as it gave him no escape when work was overly burdensome. But at times when he had only a few offers to consider, the type of investigation he hated, he used the drive home to get himself in the proper frame of mind. He often wanted to tell those who wondered if their partners were being unfaithful to simply assume they were and save him the awkward moment of revelation. Mike was never certain why this most mundane aspect of his job was more tolerable in his home environment but if it saved him from contemplating a career change it was worth a drive across town.

A newspaper under his arm and a briefcase full of customer files in his hand, Mike turned the key and entered his apartment and gasped. Paper, garbage and food cartons were scattered across every foot of the carpet. In the middle of the room, a large Irish setter sat up from his prone position and listened. He knew someone had entered, but had no idea who, as the ice cream carton he had been trying to lick the bottom of was still on his head, completely covering his eyes. The dog sat and growled softly through the wet cardboard whole-head muzzle.

Mike felt anger surge through him. "Sanford! You idiot!"

At the sound of his master's angry voice the dog yelped and the box exploded from his gaping mouth to expose the long red head of the adult setter. Now able to see, Sanford scrambled to escape to the bedroom.

"Get back here," Mike shouted, giving chase. "Why do you do this? Every stinking time! Come here!" The dog cowered in the corner and refused to make eye contact. "Come here. I mean it, Sanford. Get over here right now." Sanford shivered in fear, knowing he'd done wrong yet again but refused to willingly volunteer for punishment.

Mike surrendered and crossed the room to take the dog by the scruff of his neck and led him to the back door. The apartment had only a small balcony with a few plants and the energetic bird dog found this exile the worst of all punishments. The pet door on the balcony led to his feeder and water and his ability to use it was not in question. He simply insisted on destroying the apartment whenever unsupervised.

With Sanford dealt with, Mike set to cleaning up the garbage and disinfecting his carpet. After three years Mike had become something of an expert at eliminating odors and stains, though even after three years he still came home every day truly hopeful that his dog and merely slept and protected his home and nothing else. Imagine opening the door to find everything exactly as he had left it. That, he thought, must be a nice thing to come home to.

Coffee made and Sanford allowed back into the house, Mike thumbed half-heartedly through the pile of mounting bills. Two marked URGENT from a law firm went immediately into the trash. Logging onto his PC, he began a similar process by deleting emails unopened. He did not need to pay someone to revise his resume, he had no use for discounted Viagra and wanted nothing to do with his ex-sister-in-law or her persistent lawyers. Unwanted messages cleared, Mike scanned the remaining contacts with slightly greater interest.

One was from a familiar address and he opened it and read:
"*Mike,*

Honesty and integrity are rare enough commodities. Rarer still when you're being paid to override them. You saved me a lot more than a fortune and I'm greatly in your debt. My ex-wife and ex-partner may not agree but I owe you. Anytime I can repay, please ask.

Yours,

Paul Van Der Hausen"

That was a rare outcome for that type of investigation and it felt nice to be recognized. He perused the rest of the messages and deleted the ones he didn't like the tone of. Then he came across one which had a different look about it so he gave it a bit more attention. It took him nearly fifteen seconds to realize he was reading a message from a child. With a scoff he deleted it and moved on. To his chagrin it popped back up.

"Little hacker," he thought as he closed it. The next three messages were all from her and identical. Finally he put a block on it and its sender and reopened the email program. There was another from his sister-in-law so he read it. The message was the one he had just deleted from her, but the second paragraph mentioned a message from a child. "It's a plea for help you can't ignore. Help her, Mike. Your brother would have wanted you to."

Stunned, he deleted the message and Feryl's immediately popped up. Realizing the only way to get shed of this little hacker was to find and confront her, he responded with, "Can I help you?"

*****

Sitting across from a playground watching children was generally a dangerous thing for a man to do. But it was at the instructions of his prospective new client and he waited patiently for her to arrive.

While waiting, he pulled a candy bar from his pocket and pulled back the wrapper. The first bite was still in his mouth when Feryl approached.

"You know it's not just kids."

"What?" he managed to articulate over the chocolate and caramel.

"Chocolate. They say all kids like it. But it's mammals in general. All mammals like chocolate."

Swallowing as hard as he could, Mike cleared his mouth and extended his hand. "My dog totally agrees with you. You must be Feryl."

"Dogs like it but it's bad for them. Are you going to help me? Or just tell on me?"

"How would telling on you do either of us any good?"

"I guess that's a good answer. Do you believe my dad was murdered?"

124

"I believe those kinds of things happen, but rarely without cause. Can you think of anyone who might have had a reason to murder your father?"

"I don't know. I just know that what they say happened didn't. But it looks like it did so much the police won't look any more. That sounds like someone did it on purpose."

Mike talked to Feryl for as long as she could stay out. In the thirty five minutes they shared, he found her to be remarkably mature and knowledgeable but very imaginative and creative. The "Get to know you" period lasted far longer than he normally spent with a prospective client but this one felt different.

"So are you going to take my case?" Feryl asked.

"Legally I can't. That would require a contract and you have to be an adult to sign it. I take it you don't want you mother to sign it."

"No way, Jose."

"So I'll do this much. I'll do some digging and see if something unusual pops up. If I see something that supports your suspicions we'll talk about it and decided if there's a next step to take. Is that enough for now?"

"Do you promise to really look?"

"I can't guarantee anything and if I suspect you or anyone involved is either in danger or up to something illegal I may have to report it. But I promise to look really hard. Okay?"

"So when do I pay you?"

"For now, you can pay me by stopping the hacking thing. Just send a message and wait for an answer. Deal?"

Feryl was clearly confused. "I don't know how to hack."

Mike was practiced and spotting lies but his skill was based on adult behavior. He was truly unsure about her but she seemed sincere. "So you didn't set your message to keep popping up after I delete it?"

"I just filled out the form thing on your site."

"What about hacking into my contacts? Do you know how to do that?"

"No. Do you?"

Perplexed, Mike chose to accept her answers and move on. Something was very different about this but there was no longer any doubt he was taking the case

*****

Everett arrived home from work to find Feryl in the kitchen making a huge mess. She greeted him with a broad smile. "Hi! I'm making the dessert for supper tonight."

The smile told him he was on the right track with his parenting efforts. He was only just beginning to realize how much this meant to him. "I hope it tastes better than the kitchen looks. Your mother is going to have a fit."

"Shhh. She's upstairs cleaning. I'll clean this up before she comes down."

"Better let me give you a hand. So what are we having?"

"My very special Dan Brownies."

"Dan brownies?"

"Uh huh. See, the first time I made them everybody was all ga-ga about them and told me how great they were and everything. So I said cool and made them again. Exactly the same and everybody liked them again but they were like... yeah, these are good too. Then the third time I made them people were like... uh huh. They're good. Just like last time. Then the next time they were all... these again? It was the same exact brownies all four times but nobody got excited anymore. Guess I should try to come up with something new. Change them a bit. Huh?"

"Well, I haven't had them yet so don't change a thing. I can't wait."

"Kay. You want yours with or without hamburger?"

"Um... without."

"Good. If you said with I was going to worry about you."

"You were joking. Right?"

"Yeah. I was just joking you."

Everett found a grand smile. "Sense of humor. That's what this house was missing."

"You have one."

"Not that it was ever noticed before."

"Can I ask you something?"

"You just did."

"No, really. How do you handle her? You guys don't seem to have a lot in common."

"We used to. We actually had a lot of fun together."

Feryl nearly dropped her mixing spoon in surprise.

"Seriously. I met her when she was donating a ton of clothes to charity. She wanted to generate some attention so she organized a fashion show with the ladies at the shop. The styles were hilarious and she actually looked great."

"Mom did it, too?"

"In a bikini no less. We started talking and hit it off. Dated for a year before I popped the question."

"Where were you? Like in public and stuff?"

"Top of the Empire State Building. It was perfect. Everybody applauded when I got down on one knee and showed her the ring."

"I honestly can't imagine her being embarrassed in public. Did she say yes right away?"

"She looked down at me and smiled and said "Put your glasses on, Everett. I'm Pamela's sister."

"No way!"

"Yes way. Then she laughed and said yes. It was fun for a while."

"What changed?"

"I think I did. I moved into an administrative position in the cancer research ward at the hospital. She took the role of administrator's wife very seriously. Maybe too seriously. Used the new contacts to climb the social ladder."

"Finally something that doesn't shock me."

"True story. But she let it take over and things just got too serious too fast. Then she got seriously defensive about her past. She started making up stories about how we met and what happened to her first husband. I think that's when the fun left."

"So why don't you tell her, or at least defend yourself when she's being all mom on you and stuff?"

"Defend myself? What do you mean? Like, tell her no, or that she's wrong? Hmmm. Defiance. Bold concept. I wonder how that would go."

"It might be a good thing."

127

"It might have been at one point. But I let it go too far. Gave in too much and she only took more. Now it's too late. Anything I say, whether denial, argument, explanation or apology, only provokes her and drags it out longer. I've learned to just let it run its course."

"I don't know how you do that. I used to know somebody who was practically Gandhi. But you make Gandhi look like... well, like Mom."

"I promise you I'm not Gandhi. If I actually listened it would probably make me nuts."

"So you just stand there and not listen?"

"Just stand there. She says everything worth hearing in the first fifteen seconds so I listen that long and then run *King Kong* in my head until she's done."

"The new one?"

"Of course."

"Doesn't sound like a very good way to be married."

"To be honest, and if you repeat this I'll deny it and accuse you of stealing things, I was getting a little tired of it. But lately I feel like I'm not alone in it. I feel like I have an ally and can speak my mind... sometimes."

"You mean me?"

"Somebody else here?"

"Not really. No." She poured the chocolate batter into the pan and scraped the remains with her spoon. With the brownies ready to bake, she silently offered the mixing spoon to Everett.

He accepted the token with a smile of appreciation. "This might ruin my appetite."

"For Mom's moist-free chicken?"

He smiled. "I was beginning to wonder what it would take to get her to see how she really comes across. I don't mean hurting her feelings or being mean to her. Just somehow take a stand at just the right time and force her to stop and think."

"Maybe we can."

"Maybe you better go get cleaned up for dinner. I'll clean up the mess in here."

"Are you sure?"

"Go on. Beat it." He smiled and started gathering the mixing implements as she giggled and headed upstairs.

Pamela was in Feryl's room looking around with concern. Many of the expensive ornaments had been moved or put aside. The tastefully decorated guest room was all but lost behind the childish possessions and general preteen disarray. She set to the task of restoring some of the aesthetic value the room held before Feryl came.

The top of the nightstand was covered with books and paper and she quickly set the books on the shelf in their proper place. Then she started lifting the clothes that had been scattered around the room, thinking to herself that the clothes hamper was right there and empty. How difficult could it be? As she prepared to drop a shirt into the hamper she paused. She brought the garment to her face and smelled the fragrance of her daughter. Suddenly everything in the room smelled of Feryl and she felt very much like a mother for the first time. For this moment she enjoyed cleaning up after the precocious child. She would teach her how to care for her things. She would teach her how to be a proper young lady. Only then, as she went through the motions of mothering, did she realize she was smiling.

She picked up the clothes and put the toys and sports equipment into the closet. The closet door only partially opened as it was blocked by the large glass dome. Pamela set to moving the dome just as Feryl came in.

"No," Feryl shouted. "Don't move it!"

Pamela reeled. "Excuse me?"

"I mean please don't move it."

"I was just trying to straighten up in here. This thing takes up a lot of space."

"It's for school. If you move it, it might not work."

Pamela did not like being told what not to do. She studied the bio-dome and decided it was sufficiently complex. It might be important, so she elected to give in on this issue. "Well, dinner will be ready soon. Please get cleaned up." She left the room confident she had regained some measure of control. "And please try to keep your room a little tidier."

Feryl waited until her mother was away to confirm Uriel was unharmed and still surviving within the safe confines of the dome. "Are you okay? Did she mess anything up?"

"I'm fine, Feryl. I actually enjoyed that."

"What? Her? Why do people keep saying that?"

"I saw something very rare. She came in and her aura actually made me feel ill. It was ugly."

"Shocker. I could have told you that."

"I wish you could have seen it when she touched your shirt. It changed her. She turned almost... pleasant."

"My mom? Is she still trying to steal my jewels?"

"She was, and would if you let her. But don't stop what you're doing. Something bigger than her is coming."

"So you can see the future in auras?"

"Not the way you think. Imagine traveling down a river in a boat. The water out in front of you is pulling you along and what it hits or goes around determines what you and your boat will do. If you see it splashing around a big rock, what would you do?"

"Um. Turn? Go around the rock?"

"Exactly. And if you see a waterfall ahead?"

"Get the heck out of the river."

"Something is happening out ahead of you and it's a very bad thing. Whatever you do has to change the course of the river, even if that means getting along with your mother."

"The world is getting too weird for me."

"You'll survive. The world is always changing. Adapt with it. Make it better when you can."

"How about your world? Is the dome still protecting you against the air?"

"It's helping. I think you're helping more. I feel better when I'm with you."

"Me too. You made me normal. We're like a team. Strong when we're together. Ooh. Brownies. Can you smell that?"

"If I could this dome wouldn't be doing a very good job. Would it?"

"Trust me. They smell amazing. I wish I could bring you one."

"I wish I could taste one. It would be nice to eat a brownie before I... I need to rest now, Feryl. Watch your mother. She could surprise you."

Her tiny friend's advice was never ignored. Feryl placed her hand on the top of the glass, her way of hugging Uriel, and went downstairs for dinner.

She was first at the table and breathed in the aroma of roasted chicken. So much of her life had been spent only reading about the wondrous smells of home cooking that even the lackluster culinary talents of her mother brought forth a new experience at almost every meal.

Pamela hurried to get everything on the table while it was still hot. She called out to Everett as she set the last bowl on the table and took her seat.

"I'm here," he responded as he came into the dining room. "Do you want me to fix the drinks?"

"Everything's ready. If you would throw the chicken carcass away we could begin."

Everett picked up the platter holding the remains of the carved chicken and went to the kitchen wastebasket. Opening the lid by the floor pedal he saw it was already over-full and there was no room for the chicken so he set the platter back on the counter and took his seat at the table.

"It's full. Just leave it. I'll get it after supper."

Pamela stared in disbelief. "Just leave it? Are you serious? I'm supposed to try to enjoy my meal with a countertop covered with garbage?"

"You're supposed to not think about it for a few minutes. Don't worry. I doubt anyone is going to clean it up before I get there. It'll keep until I've eaten. Did you get some taters, Feryl?"

Pamela was becoming agitated. "It's pronounced potatoes, and someone is going to clean that up before you've had your dinner. You."

Everett gazed at her with the defiant stare she had seen only once from him and she compulsively froze, waiting for another uncharacteristic backlash. He looked just long enough to implant the thought in her that if he chose not to take out the trash he simply would not and her orders would change nothing other than the amount of breath in her lungs. Once he was sure the message had been received, Everett stood from the table and proceeded to the cupboard where they stored the trash can liners. The box was empty.

"Don't tell me we're out of bags. I specifically asked you last time we were shopping if we had any and you told me we had plenty. This is why I have to ask you two and three times. It's like talking to a—" She stopped when she saw the oddly complacent Everett heading out the door with his car keys in his hand. "Are you going to the store? Would you mind taking my car? I need to go to Bakersfield tomorrow and I won't have time to get gas. And that's another thing—"

Everett left the house to the fading sound of Pamela's voice berating him for causing all of this disruption to their evening meal. Slightly less than twenty minutes later he had completed all the necessary chores including throwing away the chicken bones. He washed his hands and sat down to a cold dinner and Pamela saying, "You always do this and then you look at me like it's my fault. I don't know why we can't just sit down and enjoy one meal like a normal family, for Feryl's sake if for no other. Is that so much to ask?"

Everett smiled at Feryl and gave her a secretive wink but said nothing.

Feryl returned the smile and started on her dessert. "Hey Everett. Tell me something. Why did they build a big old wall to keep King Kong out and then put a door in it big enough for him to walk through?"

The Last Chapter

Mike sat in dim light and scanned web pages. He had taken Feryl's word for the fact that Will was not a smoker. From there, the case was as so many. No suspects. No leads. A thin motive based mostly on Feryl's suspicions. His first step in such cases was to look at money. It was the strongest and most consistent motive for murder in human history. But he found that Will had little or no funds so he must have had something else of worth or something that would be of value in the foreseeable future. The store was heavily in debt and losing money. Few of the ingenious inventions in the store proved of any true worth. Mike wondered if anyone had been looking into his patents. His own hacker skills came into play as he tapped into a subversive watchdog website which monitored the Library of Congress. All patents, requests and queries about patents were found there with commentaries and links to forums to discuss the inventions and their political implications.

It didn't take long for Mike to find a very popular patent drawing a lot of attention. The home distillery was only one of several, but Will's was so refined and plausible that it seemed, as the conspiracy theorists phrased it, to threaten to break the thumb of the stranglehold fossil fuels held on the energy world.

The office was lit by daylight when he started and he hadn't noticed the passing of time and diminishing light. He could still see the keys and still had coffee so he pushed on, checking each name and corporation which expressed any interest in the Billings Still.

The computer screen suddenly flicked off and on. He waited as the computer slowly rebooted and hoped his search had not been lost.

"That happens sometimes." The male voice from the immediate shadows startled him but Mike maintained his composure.

"So does breaking-and-entering."

"The door's unlocked."

"And closed." Mike finally looked away from the screen and turned on the desk lamp. The new light fell on the sandy-haired stranger sitting in a chair back against the wall. "So when did you sneak in? Never mind. Why did you sneak in?"

The man smiled. "You seemed so involved, I didn't want to disturb you."

"Now that you have, how can I help you?"

"You're kind of doing it now, Michael."

"It's Mike, actually."

"I prefer Michael. Like the angel. Did you know it means God-like?"

"It means a lot of irrelevant things."

The intruder continued undaunted. "God gave Michael his own powers and sent him to earth to do away with the baddies. Doomed to failure, but what a battle he put up."

Mike feigned interest in hopes of bringing his uninvited guest to some manner of a point. "Doomed?"

"Just like Noah. He was trying to separate the good ones from the bad ones and vanquish the evil. The problem with that is good and evil resides in all of you. He couldn't surgically remove the evil without killing the host. Noah tried to leave the bad ones behind, but all it took was one human carrier of the evil gene and it grew again. Doomed. Michael didn't like losing a fight, but he realized it was impossible to separate the good from evil without killing the host, at least for him. No immortal could so thoroughly understand the complex simplicity of the human nature. It took a mortal man of uncompromising strength. One who wouldn't be corrupted by his own power. But what human could be trusted to do it? It took a while, but Michael selected a man greater than any before him. A true leader. One who could not be tempted by evil and would never rest in the search for good. This man could see the difference, so Michael gave him the power to lead good against evil on earth."

"Sounds familiar."

"The story evolved over the years. The angel became a

female and her earth became a sacred lake. The power wielded was in a sword she gave to this righteous leader."

"Now you're talking about Excalibur? King Arthur?"

"And the Lady of the Lake. Your name is Michael DeLago. Translated means Godlike or Angel of the Lake. You were the predetermined candidate, Columbo."

"I appreciate the bedtime story, but I'm kinda busy here."

"I know. You're looking into Will Billings' death. That's why I'm here. We have a mutual interest in this one."

Despite feeling no real threat, Mike instinctively became defensive. "I won't ask how you knew that. I'll just ask you to—"

"See, I agree he was murdered. But I also believe he had something I need. Something very important. I need to find that… thing, and time is a major factor."

Mike pushed away from his desk to ensure the visitor took his body language. "Even if I was a priest or a shrink, I'd still have to report any illegal act or intent. As it is, I'm a private citizen and feel obligated to tell you that you just implicated yourself in a possible homicide."

The stranger looked him directly in the eye and waved his hand like a Jedi knight. "I'm not the guy you're looking for, Michael. I need you to trust me."

In his professional experience, as well as through life lessons, Mike had never trusted anyone who specifically asked to be trusted. Especially if they'd shown a valid reason not to be trusted, which was usually the case. His instinct sent up the obligatory flags but something else came up. It was an odd sensation. Mike somehow believed the stranger. Despite having no physical reason, he could not make himself do other than trust the man. He had no real control of his emotions, but his words remained his own, and he chose them with care and logic.

"So what do you expect me to do?"

"Just keep looking. Let me help. I've got a couple of numbers which might hurry things along. You know? Let's see where it goes."

"Sorry, Charlie. I don't work and play well with others."

"Is it the money thing? It's the money. Isn't it, Michael?"

"I'm engaged. Up to my eyebrows and I don't need any help. So—"

"I do. I've been searching by every means imaginable, plus a few, but this one thing is hidden. Somehow it's been hidden and my time is running out. That's why I need your help. I've got to find it before it's too late."

"So you think Billings had this one thing and someone killed him for it?"

"I seriously doubt they knew what he had. I don't even know if he knew what it was. But if they found it, I need to know."

"Could it have been destroyed in the blast?"

"Possible. It's also possible he's the wrong guy altogether. But I have to know. So how do I buy in?"

Mike couldn't help but feel this may be a lead he had to follow. Despite the inexplicable urge to trust the stranger, he remained fearful of being too easily led, so he still tried to step slowly and retain control. "Let's start with a few questions. We'll come back to those numbers you have. First, you said 'You all have evil.' We? Why not you?"

"I meant humans."

"And that wouldn't include you?"

"Not exactly."

"I just lost interest in you."

"Your computer working yet?" His point of view gave him a view of only the back of the terminal.

Mike glanced at the screen. "Just snow. You have some sort of degausser on you?"

The man showed the palms of his hands to demonstrate he held no buttons or controls. "How about now?"

As Mike glanced again, the screen turned perfectly clear and at the very spot of his most recent search. "Good trick. You going to pull a quarter out of my ear?"

"Need more? What time is it?"

Mike looked at his wristwatch to find it had stopped. That was hard to do with Swiss Quartz, but accomplished little more than annoying him. "Okay, Svenghali. Door or window? How do you want to leave?"

"Listen. For whatever reason, you're looking for the same thing I am. Why don't we help each other and narrow the odds? What do you say, sport?"

"Out now or I call the cops."

"What do you need? More? Give me a minute. Pry your tiny mind open just that much and give me one minute to convince you, and if you still think I'm a con job I'm out like a hillbilly belly button. Just one minute. Time me on your watch, which is now working. Deal?"

Mike was annoyed and this stranger had pushed every button he had. Still, he was plagued by the sensation there was more here than he was seeing. He glanced at his wristwatch, which was indeed ticking again. "I'll give you three minutes. Cover it thoroughly. But I want nothing but truth. Fact. Any sniff of crap and the conversation ends for good. Got it?"

"Got it."

"Go."

The man adjusted himself in his chair and readied himself. "Okay. Now I said open your mind because this will stretch it. See, I'm not like you. I didn't come from where you come from. I'm here looking for something more like me than you. If I don't find it, it could be bad news for everybody."

"So you're looking for somebody. Somebody like you? One of your lot?"

"From the same source. Like part of me. Part of us. Part of... it."

"So if you're all connected, why can't you find him? Can't you feel him? Sense him? Reach out or something?"

"It's more likely a her. That's usually how it works. Don't know why. And usually I can. We all can. But I have to get close. She's small. About like that." He held up his fingers to show how tall a fairy would be. "That's hard to spot even if she's giving off signals."

"So you're looking for Tinker Bell. Beautiful."

"My time's not up." Mike sarcastically bade him continue and he did. "You're closer than you think. See, these little spark plugs have been around forever, disbursing

137

and reforming, scattering and gathering all over the place. But it's a little short sighted to think that pure energy never dies. Believe me it does. They do. They've been disappearing. Gone. Poof. That can't happen. It's like somebody parked earth and left the headlights on. Earth's battery is going dead. Or at least mankind's. This spark I'm looking for is possibly the last one. I need to find her before it's too late."

"Fairies? We're seriously talking fairies? You're really pushing it, pal."

"I warned you. And that's your word for them, and a fairly recent one at that. We've been called more names than Richard Nixon, but there hasn't been a semi-civilized race in history that didn't know about us. What's that tell you, Doc?"

"It tells me a little more about you. Nothing good."

"We... they... have been around since the earth was a molten blob. They were the heat. The energy. The electricity you've lived by since What's-his-name flew the kite."

"So you're a fairy?"

"Sort of. I'm like them, but not one of them. I'm more of a worker bee. A drone they need to walk around with you. Get and do things they can't. Call me a gatherer."

"Why? Don't they give you guys names?"

The man smiled. "Funny. No one ever asks."

"So what do I call you?"

"How about my name?"

"Which would be...?"

"Terrence."

"Terrence? Terry the Fairy?"

"Okay. I can see you're hung up on this labeling thing so I'm giving you some leash. But I gotta tell you it's getting boring, and we've got stuff to do so you need to get over it real soon. You don't want to be the guy that got his ass kicked by a fairy. Do you? You reading me, champ?"

Mike smiled. Terrence was finally speaking his language. "Reading you, Terrence. What else you got?"

"See, I'm thinking gatherer wasn't quite right. I'm more like a fireman. There's a major fire on Earth that I've been fighting for a really, really long time. There were times when

I thought I had a handle on it. But things are looking grim. If the last fairy light goes out, the fight is over."

"And you think Billings had your fairy?"

"She's not my fairy, but he's a strong candidate. It just feels right."

"Feels right? So you're like part of her. You're all energy beings like a Jedi or something. So if you're connected, I still don't get why you can't feel her."

"Are you connected? I mean to yourself? Internally. Arms, legs, lungs, pancreas and all? So why didn't you know you had cancer? Colon. Early. Not too bad, but you better have it looked at. Tick tock. Tick tock."

Mike was skeptical, but concerned enough to press. "You can see that? So fairies have X-ray vision now?"

"No. It's not that specific unless you have a lot of experience with humans. I do, ugly enough. We all have this energy field in us. Remember the electricity we were talking about? As yours is holding a lot of meat together, some is bound to be on the outside. That's what you meat-sacks call an aura. Your mental and physical state affects the intensity and color, so it's a pretty tell-tale sign."

"So you can see colon cancer in mine?"

"Just a little. Very faint. And there's something else. I just noticed it but you're… I don't know… hiding something. Odd. You're an honest guy, brutally honest, but you're lying about something. Something painful. Something you don't want anyone to know."

Mike squirmed a little but gave nothing up. "Find one person that you couldn't say that about."

"I thought I did. Good one, whatever it is. I'm going to have to keep my eye on you, Michael. In the meantime I'm seeing some acceptance in you so I'm running with it. Try to keep up."

Mike smiled and nodded in acceptance. He was still surprised at the level of trust this sarcastic stranger was drawing from him, but he kept his guard up, cautious not to divulge anything damaging. He listened intently to Terrence.

"I've been searching these imps out for eons and all it usually takes is moving around until I pick one up. They

139

used to be so thick I couldn't find a place to squat without fifteen of the little buggers climbing up my dark secret. But they started thinning a few decades ago. Thinning fast. Scary fast. It was a brush fire and we got nervous."

"We?"

"Maybe later. Stay focused here. The amount of energy being transferred is diminishing, and most of the new life is missing details. People in key spots are lacking in a quality they had before. Personality, good or bad, is being lost. Half the people in these areas don't care if the price of bread doubles or the world ends. They just stumble through their daily routines, oblivious to the world around them and the damage they are allowing by their actions or inactions."

"Democrats?"

"Not funny."

"Sorry. So what do you do when you find them? You some kind of fairy doctor?"

"No such animal. To put it in twenty-first century jargon, I take whatever data they've picked up since they first sparked and store it. When I find others, I pass the download on to them. That way they all carry a complete set of encyclopedias. Make sense?"

"So you don't actually help them at all?"

"That is helping. It's what they do and what they've been doing since the earth crusted. Ever wonder how a baby wildebeest knows to run from a lion the day it's born? Did you know that if you give a banana to a wild chimpanzee that has never seen one before, the first thing he'll do is peel it? A newborn kangaroo is less than an inch long and carries a brain the size of a dandruff flake but it will climb to its mother's teat and nurse. You think these animals read a book? It's already in them. Everything they need to know or that their ancestors learned is in them the minute they're conceived. It's how the earth keeps progressing instead of starting over each generation. But the, let's call them fairies, the fairies used to be able to do that easily. There were so many of them they couldn't help it. It was like spreading head lice at a grammar school. Recently there have been so few of them that they can't transfer the new information to each other. Species are dying. Key data is being lost. Deformities and missing elements are showing up everywhere."

"So you need to find the last of them. Can you save them?"

"Maybe. I don't know. I have to find out what's happening first. The only predator they've ever had is you guys. The last of them may be hiding from you, and that's making my job a lot harder."

Mike was almost amused at what he found himself asking, though he knew it was the most sincere emotion he'd ever expressed. "So how can I help you?"

Terrence smiled. "You're in. That's a good start. I've used every conceivable method to find her and nothing has worked. I'm drawing blanks. That's what made me think of Michael, of Noah, and of you. There's something human going on. Something new and something I'm not going to trip over. When your kind wants to find something, what do they do?"

"They call me."

"Strange as it sounds, you can think like them. You can see possibilities I might miss. I'm not saying you're smart or even normal. But between the two of us it hasn't got a chance. So there it is. You have a case before you. How would you look?"

Their plan clear, Terrence left Mike to do what he did best. He claimed he had bigger fish to fry but what could be bigger than what he had left with Mike?

The gifted investigator approached the case as he would any case. He started by ascertaining all known attributes about the subject. What did she do, need, want, like, hate, fear and think? It's nearly impossible for anything out of the ordinary to go unnoticed, and those who notice often attempt to profit from it, either by suing someone or selling the story. Once he knew what to look for, he knew what type of publication it would most likely appear in, and greed and egos generally did the hard work for you.

His search began with the one fact he had. He typed the word and began looking for fairies. The act of entering this into his computer gave the analytical sleuth reason to pause. How had he been persuaded to look for mythical creatures? Was Feryl's father involved in their demise? It was beyond unlikely for every reason he could imagine. But he had much to learn about Will Billings and Feryl, about the kind of people they were and what they could do.

Above all Mike wondered about the oddly persuasive, sandy-haired stranger that had just turned his world around. The very act of searching for fairies in a physical world seemed a reasonable act for no other reason than this man told him to. Who was he? What was he? Mike knew that his life would never be normal until he saw the end of this case, and the case was far greater than a little girl and a murdered father. Mike was no longer looking for a killer. He was looking for magic.

*****

A dozen executives sat around a mahogany conference table and starred at one another, each seemingly waiting for the other to break the silence. Finally Vic Albean spoke.

"So. If no one has anything, I suggest we break and stop meeting every Tuesday. I mean, I like doughnuts, but other than that it all seems a bit silly."

A senior gentleman at the head of the table cleared his throat before replying. "We still have things to do, Vic. What do you say we do them first?"

"What things?" asked the woman to his right.

"The merger is tied. Have we closed all the exits?"

Vic tried to keep up. "We're talking about work. Right?"

"We're talking about the people who could bring this thing down."

"It's up and running. Nothing is bigger so I'd say it's safe."

"What about competitive products?"

"Anything that even remotely seemed a threat was either purchased or shut down. We have no competition."

A small man across from Vic spoke. "There were five key people. James, Sydenham and Boyd are taken care of." No one asked him how.

"That leaves Gabriel and Cavanaugh."

"Both are resisting."

"So...?"

"Cavanaugh will be in the net by Friday. He's worried about his family or something."

Vic looked up. He felt that should have meant something to him. The family comment was something he used to have to take into account when dealing with people. He found it odd that he no longer could recall why.

"And Gabriel?" asked the head.

Everyone in the room looked to Vic.

"I practically put her on a plane. She'll be in Barbados on Friday."

"And?"

"And I truthfully don't need to know more than that. Can I go now?"

*****

Karen munched celery sticks while she populated her spreadsheet with costs and profit curve projections for her new project. The meeting with the chemical suppliers went better than expected and she was nearly ready to take the forced vacation Global Nortatem had been pushing her toward since the ink dried on the palm oil merger contracts.

She hoped she could slip out without being noticed. This way she could insist she was away longer than she actually was and could get back to insuring her future security all the quicker. Even as she pulled figured from one list to another, central sheet, something in the impending trip felt wrong. She knew something more than the merger was going on and she had been deliberately excluded. Moreover, she knew something was altering everyone around her. The closer they were to the project, the more noticeable the change.

It bothered her but not so much as to put her off her own schedule. Karen had a personal rule of never dwelling on things she could not affect. So many of her rules had been relaxed recently but she forced herself to ignore it all and forge ahead. Despite the growing lack of focus, despite the fear of having no job to return to, despite the impending sense of dread, she would take her laptop and head off to the beach. Something or someone wanted her there and she would resist them no more.

Sunlight beamed in through the bedroom window, filtered by the sheer curtains. The life-giving energy warmed and cleansed the air in Uriel's dome. Each time she felt herself slipping away something brought her back. First it was the caring touch of a truly sensitive child. Next it was the need to help that child. When Feryl gave her the protective dome, the tiny fairy was shielded from all that was harmful in the world of humans and the world was shielded from her. The heavy, reflective glass denied her the ability to feel outside or be felt. She was safe.

Not far enough away, Terrence stood and felt the air. He touched everything in the world and searched his senses for any trace of the tiny spark that continued to flicker, out there somewhere. She had to be there or he had no meaning. She had to be found. The future of life on earth demanded it. He would not rest until he found out who was protecting her. Nothing could stand between him and the last fairy.

XXX

When was the last time you were reading a good book and found a completely different story developing in your mind? This happens to me quite often. I'll be well into an engrossing novel and find myself wondering why the heroine doesn't just stop trying to win an argument with him and simply leave him (*preferably after smacking him in the head with a lamp*). She's young, intelligent and strong of character. Surely she could do better than a womanizing, gambling fraud who takes all of his frustrations out on her. But what if she did and found the world of single women to be a bit frightening? What if she found it too difficult to let go of the opulence he provided? What if she sought to find love only to learn she was gay? What if she found true love but he was a werewolf?

And so the new story rivals the text for my attention and by the time I finish my novel I've got a version Jeffrey Archer never imagined. New stories can come from anywhere. My wife used to think it bothered me when she suggested alternate story lines for the characters in my books. Being Irish, she soon spoke her mind anyway and found that I loved her ideas (*most of the time, well some of the time, well once*) and praised her for making me a better writer.

Some time ago she suggested an elaborate story line for a book inspired by an image I did of a dying fairy. It was merely a whim but she liked the artwork and we talked for hours about what might have killed her and whether or not a person could find or even know about a dead fairy. I liked the idea but told her I wouldn't be able to start on it for at least a year. She insisted and I told her to write it herself. The instant the words left my lips I realized my mistake and leapt for cover for fear of "the look", begged her forgiveness for my unfortunate phrasing and bought her something nice. I did eventually agree and with no small measure of input from her and despite it being different from anything I had ever written before, I wrote it.

As soon as I began writing it, she asked me what kind of book I thought this would be. Was it a fantasy? A mystery? An action/thriller/romance/comedy/drama? As with all of my works at this stage, I had no idea how to answer. The problem I have with genre fiction, if you can call it a problem (though I can't imagine any artist agreeing), is that I write entirely from inspiration, and that inspiration comes from a variety of sources. While readers tend to look for a favorite genre first, writing starts from the other end. If my next story turned out to be an erotic period novel, the readers of that genre might see me as the new guy on the block.

In most cases an author simply has something to say that he or she feels the world, or at least a sampling of the population, might want to hear. The basic story was there but lacked any real substance. It needed a foundation that would matter to a broad audience. For this, I had to look no farther than the evening news. So many issues were emerging it was difficult to choose one, so I let it choose me. The environment has always been a concern of mine, and the more I delve into the individual issues the more they draw me in. I feel at once frightened, angered, confused and even guilty when I look at the staggering rate at which we as voracious humans are depleting the earth's natural resources. War, famine, recession, Pierce Brosnan singing and all other human atrocities take a back seat, as it would be of little comfort to have a healthy, peacetime economy if we were all dead.

We probably won't destroy the planet. The earth is just a big rock floating in space and it will still be floating long after we're gone. The only thing we're destroying is the earth's ability to support life. We were fortunate enough to develop on this planet, but we are also advanced enough to know how fragile our existence here is. We continue our insatiable ways as though we can do no permanent harm to the land, sea, air and ozone layer despite the abundance of clear and irrefutable evidence to the contrary. Anything with a beginning must have an end, and we are more than capable of hastening that end. We deplete forty percent of the ocean's bounty annually. We burn and mishandle fossil fuels that poison the sea and the air. We slaughter endangered species to extinction and bulldoze their native habitat in order to plant comparatively useless crops. It would appear even to us that we are deliberately self-destructive. In truth, we don't hate tigers or dolphins. We don't dislike the rainforests, and we would love to see the oceans clean and bountiful for generations to come. We contradict all of these messages for one reason. Profit. Humans are greedy. We want more of everything. We risk dumping oil into the oceans because we can sell it if we don't. We scrape the ocean floor with massive nets, killing everything we find, in hopes that some of the fish we kill are marketable. We destroy the forests that have been home to thousands of species because palm trees yield palm oil and we can sell that. Why? Why would we do this? It's not short-sightedness, as we see what we're doing. It's not stupidity, as it takes a highly intelligent and creative species to do this much damage this quickly and efficiently. It's pure madness, because we do it anyway.

There, in that madness, I found my story. The beginning of the foreseeable end of all things. That is what I care most about, and that needs to be said again and again in so many ways and genres and mediums that no one can honestly claim they didn't know. I don't know if we can change. But I would never feel at ease if I did not at least try. I like the world and I hate that we're ruining it. So I wrote about that, and about a dying fairy.

In the next book, The Fairy Hunters, Feryl is back and the gift she received from Uriel has changed everything. But if turning over a single grain of sand on a beach can change the course of history, what impact can result from an act the magnitude of such an act as Uriel's gift?

The frail girl had spent ten years of her life at death's door. Abandoned by her mother at infancy because of her illness and robbed of any hope of normality, Feryl was what she had made herself, the combination of the hand she had been dealt and the strength of character to rise above it. When her father was brutally murdered, the eleven-year-old girl was left almost alone. She had her cold hearted mother and her step father, and she had her fairy. Uriel healed her with her touch, then Feryl saved Uriel with her knowledge of illness'. Finally Uriel gave her young savior the greatest gift of all. She gave her the strength to live through the loss of her father and the will to push on.

Karen Gabriel knew she had done something big, but she could not have known where the devastating juggernaut would take her. The closer the people around her were to the "project" the more they seemed to change. It was as though they were being drained of their personality, their humanity, everything that made them unique.

147

But some zeal had survived in the corporate plan. Karen had served her purpose and she now was expendable, even dangerous. But Karen Gabriel was not one to lose a fight without so much as throwing a punch. Even the mega-giant corporation with seemingly unlimited resources, power, international influence and tentacles long enough to strangle entire countries could not intimidate this woman. She had to find a way to hit back, expose their weakness and take them down. An impossible task for a lone warrior. She would need an ally.

Enter Mike DeLago, a private investigator with more integrity than resources. Feryl had decided to hire him to uncover the truth surrounding her father's death and thus drew him into the stream of mystery and intrigue that would claim lives and change history. This loner in work and in life would need an ally if this case was to end favorably.

Mike knew what to look for thanks to the appearance of a mysterious and oddly persuasive stranger that seemed to be everywhere and anywhere. With an unnatural knowledge of the nature of the planet and little more than disdain for the human race, Terrence was on a mission and would not be stopped. He was the best at what he did but even this natural hunter knew when he was outmatched. Time and an unseen force stood between him and his quarry and the fate of the human race hung in the balance. Terrence chose to take a step never before considered. He recruited an ally.

Each of the hunters, Karen, Mike, Terrence, were unknowingly being drawn together for one reason. Feryl had a fairy.

Be braced for a new level of excitement, danger, intrigue and heart-warming emotion as the characters from the first book return on a mission to survive against all odds in **The Fairy Hunters**.

148

Missouri born **Donovan Galway** spent much of his youth a slave to his rambling bone. After a short stint in the Navy, he moved to Phoenix where he studied Broadcast Journalism at ASU. He soon shifted his interests to literature and took courses in creative writing.

As with most first novels, his was unpublishable and he elected to keep writing as a hobby and forged an unhappy career in banking. Nearly two decades later, he met a woman in Ireland who took notice of his hobby and convinced him to publish one of his works. Galway published two books in print-on-demand, moved to Ireland, married the woman and has been writing ever since.

Donovan Galway presently resides in Northern Ireland with his wife, traveling to the U.S. occasionally. He is a lover of classical music as well as rock, (*the only music he doesn't like is accordions, marching bands, bagpipes and gospel*) and enjoys the theatre and the classics in all forms.